Ivan Vladislavić

. . .

THE
FOLLY

archipelago books

First Archipelago Books Edition, 2015

First published as *The Folly* by David Philip Publishers, South Africa, in 1993.

Archipelago Books
232 3rd Street #A111
Brooklyn, NY 11215
www.archipelagobooks.org

Library of Congress Cataloging-in-Publication Data
Vladislavić, Ivan, 1957-
The Folly / Ivan Vladislavić. – First Archipelago Books edition.
pages ; cm
ISBN 978-0-914671-37-4 (pbk. : alk. paper)
I. Title.
PR9369.3.V57F65 2015
823'.914–dc23   2015013044

Cover art: Jean Dubuffet

Archipelago Books gratefully acknowledges the generous support from
Lannan Foundation, the New York State Council of the Arts, a state agency,
and the New York City Department of Cultural Affairs.

PRINTED IN THE UNITED STATES OF AMERICA

Distributed by Penguin Random House

FOR MINKY

THE
FOLLY

Nieuwenhuizen stood on the verge, in the darkness, looking down the street. In one hand he held a brown imitation-leather portmanteau; in the other some small, cold coins given to him by a taxi-driver moments before. The tail-lights of the taxi flared up at the end of the street, and vanished.

Nieuwenhuizen turned to the plot. It was smaller than he'd been led to believe, no more than an acre, and overgrown with tall grass and weeds. The land was bounded on two sides by an unruly hedge, breaking against the night sky, and on a third by a prefabricated cement wall with panels in the shape of wagon-wheels. The fourth side, where he found himself, had once been fenced off from the street: the remains of this frontier – crumpled scrolls of barbed wire, a gate, some club-footed wooden posts in concrete boots – lay all around. He tightened his grip on his change with one hand and on the sponge-swaddled handle of his portmanteau with the other, high-stepped over a tangle of wire, and pushed through the grass, onwards.

Sour dust burst from the brittle stems he felled and crushed with his boots. Breathing the dust down, salivating, swallowing, he fixed his eyes on the horizon and forged ahead. After a while he stumbled over an anthill. It seemed a pity to waste this discovery, so he stood on top of the hill and turned his face ceremoniously to the four corners of his inheritance. It was a big face, with a crack of a mouth and a stump of a nose, with unfathomable sockets, craggy brows and a bulging forehead dented in the middle, altogether suited to the play of moonlight and shade. His survey revealed a single tree in the elbow of the hedge, and he chose that spot for his camp.

Nieuwenhuizen hung his scarf on a thorn. Then he sat on his portmanteau under the tree and looked expectantly at the bloodshot windows of the house behind the wagon-wheel wall.

In the lounge of this house Mr and Mrs Malgas, the owners, were watching the eight o'clock news on television.

"Here we go again," said Mr Malgas when the unrest report began, and he turned the sound off by remote control.

At that very moment there appeared on the screen a burning shanty made of split poles, cardboard boxes and off-cuts of chipboard, and patched with newspaper and plastic bags. It was hemmed in on all sides by a great many shanties just like it, except that, for one reason or another, none of these others were burning.

"This is nothing," Mrs Malgas said gloomily. "Just you wait. The worst is yet to come."

Whereupon she darted out of her Gomma Gomma armchair, snatched Mr's plate from his TV tray, swept two vertebrae off it into a smudge of fat on her own plate, rattled two knives and smote them down ostentatiously, gnashed two forks with shreds of mutton and grains of rice caught between their teeth, dropped crumpled serviettes on top of the wreckage, slid the empty plate underneath the full one, set both down on the coffee-table and returned to her seat (in one florid motion).

"Where is everybody?" Mr asked.

The shack was still burning. Tattered curtains of flame blew out of the windows and columns of smoke rose from holes in the walls where the patches had burnt away. The smoke went straight up into the heavens. The image blurred and vibrated, then composed itself again. Next, the roof, which was made of corrugated iron and weighted with stones, brought the entire structure crashing down in a silent outburst of sparks and embers. Among the charred boards the camera disclosed an iron bedstead, the red-hot spirals of an inner spring mattress, and a padlocked tin trunk. Then it pointed out a pair of smouldering boots.

Mrs Malgas stared at the boots.

Mr Malgas, who owned a hardware shop, focused on one of the corrugated sheets and remarked, "Beautiful piece of iron."

"Shhh!"

While he was trying to gather kindling in the dark, Nieuwenhuizen tripped over his anthill again and measured his length on the ground. As he was picking himself up his hand chanced to fall on an object concealed in the grass. He extricated it excitedly. It was an old oil drum, twenty-five litres approx., hacked open crudely at one end, somewhat distended at the other. He shook some sand and grass out of it, clamped it under one arm and thumped its bottom into shape with his fist. He tilted it in the moonlight. For all its blemishes, it seemed brim-full of potential – a smidgen of which he was pleased to realize immediately: he carried his paltry collection of twigs in it as he tramped back to camp.

It would be pleasant to sit on a stone, he thought, but he couldn't find one of the right shape or size, so he up-ended the drum and sat on that instead. He swept together a pile of dry leaves. Then he shuffled the twigs into a faggot and broke them in half.

The splintering of the wood made him suppose, for an instant, that he was breaking his own fingers into kindling, and the idea made him queasy. He flourished his hands to see whether they were still in working order. Reassured, he raked the scattered metacarpi and phalanges into a nest and dropped a match on them.

The frog squatted in a milky pool at the bottom of the mug, staring up with one glassy eye. Mr Malgas spooned instant-coffee granules over it and scalded it with boiling water. It didn't bat an eyelid.

The frog-mug had been bought at a sale of factory rejects, and for that reason it was Mrs Malgas's favourite, warts and all. Mr Malgas thought it was in bad taste. He stirred the coffee, scraping the frog on the murky bottom maliciously with the spoon. He fished the tea-bag out of his own mug, which was chocolate-brown and had I ♥ DIY printed on it in biscuit. He thought this one was gimmicky too, but it had been a Father's Day present from his spouse and he used it out of a sense of duty. He squashed the bag flat against the spoon with his thumb to extract the essence of the flavour and dropped it in the bin next to the stove. He jammed one forefinger through the thick ears of both mugs, scooped up three buttermilk rusks – one for the Mrs and two for himself – and switched off the kitchen light with his elbow.

In the darkness, in the doorway, an unaccustomed smell prickled his nostrils. Drums boomed. A burning shack caved in, predictably, in the back of his mind. He sniffed, filtering the intruder from the haze of home cooking and pine-scented air-freshener.

Wood-smoke.

"Sigh!"

He put everything down again and wiped a porthole in the misted glass of the window above the sink. Nieuwenhuizen's fire waved its small hands in the far corner of the plot next door. An intimate relationship between the flames and his own palm circling on the glass came unbidden into Mr Malgas's mind and caused a shameful pang in his chest.

"Mrs!"

She recognized the tone: summonsing. It was the one he used when he wanted her to drop what she was doing and hasten into his presence, when he needed her to bear witness to one of his trivial observations. What could it be this time? A rusk with a human profile? Something beastly in the milk? A bubble on the end of the tap? A cobweb? A stick-insect on the outside of the glass?

"Mrs!"

There was a note of urgency in his voice. Perhaps he'd snagged his pullover on something? But as usual she mumbled, "Ja."

"Come here a second."

"Coming." An actress Mrs had seen before playing a victim in a human drama looked at her through the bottom of a mixing-bowl and assured her that it was clean. Mrs rose resentfully and went to the kitchen.

Mr enlarged the porthole in the windowpane with a dishcloth and she peered through it.

The flames wavered.

"What did I tell you?" she said knowingly. "It was an omen. Where there's smoke there's fire." Then, baffled by his apprehensive silence, she went on in a stage whimper, "Shall I call the fire brigade?"

"There's someone there, tending it," he answered. "A man, I think."

At once a tall figure passed in front of the fire, casting a gigantic shadow over their house.

"Shall I call the cops?" she asked wistfully.

At that instant the fire vanished. Nieuwenhuizen, who was about to retire for the night, had turned his drum over the flames to snuff them.

Mr and Mrs Malgas looked into the night with the disquieting feeling that they had imagined something.

Nieuwenhuizen lay on his back, resting his head on a corner of the portmanteau and his feet on the drum, which radiated the deep inner warmth of the coals. He gazed up through the branches of his tree, and saw a wrinkled moon skewered on a thorn.

The ground shifted. He spread his arms, he unfurled the fingers of each hand and crooked them, he rootled them into the grass, massaging, until his fingertips touched the subsoil and, by the gentlest of pressures, steadied the lurching surface.

Then he allowed his head to topple so that his eyes fell once again on the house beyond the wagon-wheel wall. In a frosted oval, on curly vines of burglarproofing, two bruised, abashed faces hung ready to fall.

Burning rubber!

Mr lay covered up like a dead pedestrian. Mrs traced the outlines of his sharp hip-bone, his rounded shoulder and his blunt skull under the blankets. She switched out the light, fumbled for the fading image of the bed and slipped into it with a shudder.

At least the body was warm. She attached herself to his flannelled back and kicked his heels to make room on the hot water bottle. The warm air trapped under the bedclothes smelt of lemon-scented towelling, surgical gloves and Vicks Vaporub. She reached over his hip, slipped her hand under his pyjama jacket and pressed it into the unctuous, aromatic flesh of his belly.

"Hands off!" he commanded, sucking in his paunch and shivering. She clenched her fists obediently.

Nieuwenhuizen arose at dawn, shrugging off sheets of newspaper and blankets of grass. He scummed the ashes from his fire and scooped a hollow in the warm coals at its core. From the portmanteau he retrieved an aluminium-foil parcel containing his breakfast, and embedded it in the coals.

Only then did he lift his eyes to survey his new dominion.

He liked it. Its contours and dimensions were just right, and so too were its colour schemes and co-ordinates, not to mention its vistas and vantage-points. The sheer cliffs of the hedge towering at his back, dappled with gold and amber, tapering into the far-off haze on either side; the vast and empty sky, baby-blue on the horizon, and sky-blue in the middle distance, and navy-blue in the dome above; the veld rolling away before him in a long blond swell, reefed by the shadows of the hedge and stirred by a breath of wind, swirling now through thickets of shrubs and weeds, spilling now over rocks, boiling into heathery foam, spending itself at last against the wagon-wheel wall in the distance – all these things pleased him enormously.

The house behind the wall pleased him less. It was of a pasty, pock-marked complexion, and there were rashes of pink shale around the windows, which were too close together and overhung by beetle-browed eaves. What thoughts were rattling in these unhappy head-quarters?

In the cold light of day it was clear to Mr and Mrs Malgas that they had not been seeing things. The man they had glimpsed the night before was still there, as large as life – a little bit larger, in fact, as Mr Malgas remarked.

Mr was woken soon after dawn by the beating of drums. He lay still, listening fearfully to this wild music and the wilder counterpoint of his heartbeat. The drumming grew louder, closer, more frenzied – and then revealed itself to be hammering. He knew at once where it was coming from. He spilled out of bed and put on his dressing-gown.

Mrs watched through lowered lids as he punched his arms through the sleeves of his gown and crept noisily from the room. When he was gone she reached for the clock and brought its expressionless face close to her own. Then she pressed in the knob that switched off the alarm and pulled the blankets over her head. She was engulfed at once by the saline backwash of Mr's sleep and tumbled headlong into dream-land.

Meanwhile, Mr stole in his socks through the grey light, over a springy pasture of carpet, past the velvety humps of armchairs asleep on their feet, to a window that offered a good view of the terrain.

The stranger was pitching a tent made of bright-red canvas in the corner under the tree. Mr was struck by his pitching method, which was unusual, to say the least. Unusual? Why, it was probably without precedent. Briefly: he pounded the tent-pegs into the ground with a stone, according to the dictates of a worksong that he piped out in a reedy voice, wheezing and clouding the air with his breath. Between each blow he paused in an attitude of intense expectation, with the stone held high above his head, waiting for a signal from his singsong melody. Then he allowed the stone to fall, so that his hand, rather than propelling it, seemed to be dragged down by it. The impact of the stone on the head of the peg caused him to fly into the air like a marionette, with all his limbs jangling.

Between pegs Nieuwenhuizen stood up to stretch his back and to watch out of the corner of his eye, and the impression Mr had gained the night before that he was unusually tall and thin was confirmed: it had not been a trick of the firelight. He was wearing a khaki safari suit a few sizes too big for him and a pair of home-made boots with tyre treads, which accentuated how long and stringy his legs were.

When Mrs resurfaced it was light in the room. She glanced at the clock and saw that she had been sleeping for an hour and ten minutes. The house was silent. She rose and went to fetch her gown from its hook behind the door. Through the doorway she saw Mr as a dark stain on the bright gauze of the lounge window.

Nieuwenhuizen ambled along in the shadow of the hedge. His boots smashed down frost-brittled forests of grass and branded crosses and arrows on the tender skin of the soil. He counted the paces under his breath. At the same time he wondered what kind of hedge this was. It was shedding its leaves: what good was that? He paused to look at a dimpled berry resting in the fork of a branch. He had never seen anything like it. Perhaps this plant was a member of the berry family rather than the hedgerow as such? He pincered the berry between horny nails and stepped off again. Stopped. He'd lost count. He shook a branch of the hedge petulantly, scattering a flock of feathery leaves, plucked one out of the air as it settled, crushed it to snuff between thumb and forefinger, and snorted it gingerly. Ah!

"I've pitched a few tents in my time," Mr said to Mrs over breakfast a little later. "I'm the adventurous type as you know, I've been in some out-of-the-way places – but I've never seen anything like this. Totally unorthodox. Come away from that window."

Mrs didn't budge. She watched the stranger browsing, lifting his big feet and putting them down deliberately, staring at the ground. His long limbs and knobbly joints fascinated her. Clip-clop. He had the gait of a buck, lazy, double-jointed. "What kind of a tent did you say it was?" she asked.

"A two-man tent."

"Exactly. That's what's bothering me. There's only one of him. What does he want with a tent for two men?"

"He's quite tall."

"Go on, defend him. But mark my words: He's bad news. I can smell it a mile off." She tossed back the lank ear-flaps of her hair and turned up her nose, displaying to good effect two well-formed, flared nostrils, like inverted commas.

"Perhaps he likes to have a bit of space around him. Some people are like that."

"I still say we should call the cops. If it's the wide open spaces he wants, let them put him on a train to the platteland."

Mr scalped his egg and stirred its soft-boiled insides with the point of his knife. Between a thick brown forefinger and thumb he took up a slim white finger of buttered bread (it was margarine, to tell the truth), dunked it in the egg, wiped it carefully on the rim of the shell and raised it dripping to his lips. He chewed and said, "Now I don't want you doing anything foolish while I'm at work."

"It's all very well for you. You don't have to sit here all day long putting up with him."

"Sigh!"

"I wish you wouldn't say that!"

"Say what?"

"Sigh. It's irritating."

He picked up the chopped-off lid of eggshell on the end of his thumb. It looked like a miniature skull-cap stuck to a fillet of white flesh.

Nieuwenhuizen extended his right hand, clasped a branch of the hedge and shook it warmly.

"What if he's a dangerous criminal?" she went on. "Perhaps he's on the run."

"If he was on the run he wouldn't be standing out there in broad daylight making a racket. Come away from the window." She came away.

"You always think the worst of people. He could just as well be a professor, fallen on hard times. If I had to hazard a guess, that's what I'd say. Just look at the head he's got on him! When I behold that head I must say it gives me a good feeling about him, here, in the pit of my stomach." He pointed out the spot with the yellow tip of his knife.

Mrs slumped down at the table and gazed into the frog's eye, which gazed back without blinking from the gummy dregs of her coffee. "Is he one of these squatters we've been hearing so much about? Will he put up a shack and bring hundreds of his cronies to do the same? 'Extended families.' What do you think? Will they hammer together tomato boxes and rubbish bags, bits of supermarket trolleys and motor cars, noticeboards and yield signs, gunny sacks and jungle gyms, plastic, paper, polystyrene . . ."

"Enough."

". . . brass, bronze and Beaverboard. Fine. We'll be forced out of our home. They'll play their radios loud. They'll go in the streets like dogs. They'll tear up our parquet for firewood."

Nieuwenhuizen dug a moat around his tent with a broken bottle. Then he reviewed the interior of his portmanteau, in which a wide range of utensils and provisions lay snugly, cushioned by underpants, vests, and socks rolled into balls and swallowing their own toes. His rummaging fingers scared up a mouldy smell, which reminded him of the furry bodies of moths, which in turn brought the unthinkable taste of them into his mouth. To dispel this loathsome impression he quickly unpacked a few things and arranged them to his satisfaction around the camp. It looked good. Now for furniture. He fetched stones and constructed a simple table and chairs, and a hearth with nifty inglenooks and ledges.

He rested.

While he was lolling on his stony seat the man of the house emerged. Nieuwenhuizen followed his progress by the roar of an engine, gears grating, gates clanging, a door slamming. Soon a battered bakkie with a home-made canopy and a built-in roof-rack piled with planks and a capsized wheelbarrow came slowly but surely into view. Bravo! Right on cue. There was a sign on the door – half a manikin, Mr . . . Something . . . the surname was obscured by a smear of red paint. The bakkie drew up at the kerb. The driver got out, walked ponderously to the rear of the vehicle and kicked the tyre, and looked at his toe-cap. Then he went to the front, kicked that tyre, and looked at his shoe again. Then he got back into the cab and drove off.

Long after the sound of the engine had died away Nieuwenhuizen remained glued to his chair with his head cocked and his mouth hanging open. Then he roused himself with an effort. There was work to be done.

To begin with, he ruled lines with his eyes, from one little landmark to another, twig to knoll and kerbstone to leaf, pillar to post and branch to berry, so that his territory lay enmeshed in a handsome grid, and he numbered the blocks methodically, Roman numerals down one side and capital letters down another, and spent hours plundering each one until it delivered up its riches. He was surprised at how many useful objects lay concealed in the grass: beer bottles and cold-drink tins, inner tubes, bits of board and metal, scribbles of wire, insulators, screws, plastic bags, cardboard cartons – well, there was only one: a cardboard carton, strictly speaking – and scraps of newspaper. He carried all his finds back to camp in his drum and stored them away for future reference. He also salvaged half a dozen fine fence-posts and a cast-off letter-box shaped like a shoe.

The discovery that pleased him most was a weathered FOR SALE notice he disentangled from the barbed-wire shroud of the fence. He was so delighted with it that he made a note of its position on the grid (XA) and wished he'd had the foresight to do the same for the other items. He turned it over in his hands. He gave it a stiff kick to dislodge some of its rust. It had useful object written all over it. It was not long before a precise potential function revealed itself: with the addition of a few strategically placed holes this simple metal plate would make an excellent braai-grille.

At midday he sought the spiky shade of his thorn-tree, made himself comfortable, and scoured every last flake of rust and blistered paint off the sign with handfuls of gravel and an ingenious barbed-wire brush of his own device. Then he set about punching holes through it in regular rows with a large nail, which he had brought with him, and a well-proportioned flint, recently acquired, which he had nominated as his hammer.

He now found time to reconsider his first impressions of his new neighbour. He was not disappointed. Firstly, he assumed that the tyre-kicking performance had been for his benefit, which was a sure sign that the man was eager to make contact. Secondly, the man worked, or so he inferred from the rattletrap vehicle and businesslike demeanour. Thirdly, his physical presence was imposing. He was bulky and solid. His face was the colour of putty, but his forearms were a healthy kiaat-red. Shirt-sleeves in this weather? Either he was hard as nails or he was trying to impress. His head was a little square perhaps, and his hair plastered down on its flat top like a doormat, but his features were open and friendly. No one's perfect.

Then there was the woman. Nieuwenhuizen didn't know quite what to make of her. There was no sign of her now, but a few times that morning he had seen her face rise wanly behind a mist of net curtaining or sink below the horizon of a window-sill.

My next-door neighbours, he thought, except that I have no door.

In mid-afternoon, when his handiwork was almost done, his eye fell for the hundredth time on the prefabricated wall – and he noticed with a jolt that the wagon-wheel panels were interspersed with rising suns. He was still puzzling over how these panels had escaped his attention thus far when it struck him, with another jolt, that perhaps they were setting suns! And who could tell?

This line of thought threw him into a state of violent scepticism about every perception he had had since his arrival in this godforsaken place. He examined the house behind the wall with new interest. It was still there, which was reassuring, but would its plastered features pass for white? More like off-white, you could even say cream. Buttermilk? As for the roof, that was red all right, but what kind of red? Raspberry? It was certainly not the same shade as the bougainvillaea creeping up one pillar of the stoep. Hang on. What's this? Flowering out of season? The blooms looked as if they were made of crinkle-paper pinched on stems like pipe-cleaners. That would be *her* doing. He turned his eyes on the empty frames of the windows, and the curtains on either side, nipped into hourglasses by tasselled thongs, and tried to caption them: Kitchen. Lounge. Bedroom. Bathroom? Bedroom. Lounge. Two lounges?

Mrs Malgas, who had been standing thinly behind a lamp in her lounge for more than an hour, transfixed by the stranger's peculiar mode of hammering, was astonished when his legs suddenly shot out rigidly in front of him. His kneecaps bounced up and down as if they were mounted on springs and his head bobbed as if it belonged to a doll. He looked for all the world like a dummy manipulated by an amateur ventriloquist. Abruptly he slumped against the tree trunk and appeared to fall asleep. But then he jumped again, causing his heels to thud together with such force that one of his boots flew off.

Now he turned his eyes on her so intently that she was sure he had discovered her presence. She fled to her bedroom and lay down until she felt herself again. She switched on the radio. A familiar voice promised to tell her how to remove bloodstains from fine linen, stay tuned, and reminded her that the devil finds work for idle hands. In response she took one of Mr's socks from her sewing basket, a brick-red woollen sock thick as a blanket, stretched it over a fused light-bulb that served as a darning-egg so that the hole in its heel yawned, matched a length of wool to the colour and threaded a needle.

Do NOT soak b-s item in water, neither h nor c – will set stn. Sqz juice 1 lemon in tmblr & stir well. Fold in white 1 L. egg & 1 Tsp Bicarb. Sprnkl.

When she had finished darning the sock she put everything away in the basket and lay looking up at the ceiling and dozing. The radio hinted and tipped. Time passed. A time-check. Time to start the supper. She spilled a cup of rice on the Formica top of the kitchen table and picked through it. Then she swept the broken and discoloured grains into the palm of her hand and carried them to the bin. She stood on the pedal to open the lid, and at the same time pushed open the window and scattered the grains into the bed of gazanias below. The stranger was nowhere to be seen, although his tent was glowing like a lantern in the dusk.

Nieuwenhuizen turned his hands over in the rosy air and watched the play of light on his thick veins. Through the fretwork of his fingers he saw the unaccustomed lightning of thorny branches against the canvas. The walls swayed as he breathed, in and out, and despite himself he began to drift off. He turned his big head heavily on his pillow, which was nothing more than a plastic bag stuffed with straw, and it crackled. He threw himself over on his stomach, pressed his face into the din, and spread his arms and legs until each of his extremities was wedged firmly in one of the four corners of the tent.

"All day, he was pacing up and down like a lunatic in a cage," said Mrs, "stepping on his shadow and picking up junk. Like so." She gave a demonstration of Nieuwenhuizen's rickety stride. "And then he was hammering, *bof-bof-bof,* for three hours on end. I nearly went up the wall." She demonstrated the hammering too, rattling her hands and nodding her head. "And then, to crown it all, he went like this – twice!" She sat down in a Gomma Gomma armchair and gave two startling imitations of Nieuwenhuizen's spasms.

Mr was perplexed. He stared at his wife's shaggy slippers, sitting up like dogs on the ends of her stiff legs, and couldn't think of anything to say.

"You might have phoned, just to see if I was coping."

While Mrs was dishing up the supper, Mr kept watch in the darkened lounge. The camp, alone on the moon-bleached veld, with the hedge bearing down on it like a wave about to break, appeared to him as an island of light and warmth. The stranger crouched over his cooking-fire. A hurricane-lamp suspended from a branch overhead buttered his shoulders lightly, and the coals splashed blood on his down-turned face. A screen of smoke drifted over the landscape and softened all its edges.

He eased a window open, put his face to the burglar-bars and sniffed the meaty breeze. Scrumptious. He was still standing there with his hands in a knot behind his back and his nose quivering when she carried in their plates, drew the curtains in front of his eyes and switched on the TV.

"The rice is dry," she said. "I can't concentrate with all this going on."

"I've been studying our friend and his camp," said Mr as they ate. "It looks quite jolly." He was thinking, too, that it looked almost – what? . . . Brave. But the contemptuous dimple in one corner of her mouth warned him against voicing that observation and he remarked instead, "We should have a braai one of these days."

"In this weather?"

They both chewed and stared into the TV set, where they saw the same collapsing shanty they had seen the night before, now captioned ARCHIVE MATERIAL. Mrs shivered and put her hand in Mr's. His fingers remained open, like an unsprung trap. She put her fork down and curled his fingers over one by one with her free hand.

Mr reappraised the iron roof, which fell interminably in slow motion. He picked up his fork in his left hand and said, "This is delicious. Fit for a king. Never mind a king – an emperor."

. . .

Nieuwenhuizen lifted a chop from a polystyrene tray on the end of a piece of wire, carried it up to his nose and sniffed it. Full of goodness. He dropped it on the grille. He sprinkled the blood from the tray over the chop and suspended his hungry face in the smoke. Then he sat down with a sigh on one of his hard chairs.

He looked at the windows of the house behind the wall and tried to imagine what the occupants were doing. He saw Mrs at a wooden sideboard lighting a candle in a stainless-steel candlestick. He saw Mr, in slippers and gown, glass in hand, pipe in mouth, darkening a doorway. She fluttered at the wick. He stepped out of the door-frame into the warm embrace of the candle-light. He took two steps towards her, and paused. She looked over her shoulder, and smiled. He put one hand on the back of a chair and raised the other towards her hair. He stopped. He would go no further.

Nieuwenhuizen lanced the chop with his wire and flipped it over. He looked at the windows of the house and tried again.

Mr stepped out of the frame and took two steps towards Mrs. The ruby liquid in his glass glinted. She looked over her shoulder, which was sheathed in crimson taffeta, padded within and sequinned without, brought the match up to her mouth and blew out the flame. A puff of smoke drifted into his eyes. He blinked rapidly, put one hand on the back of the chair and raised the other towards her lips, which still held the softly rounded shape of her breath. His hand hung in the air, O! He would go no further.

Nieuwenhuizen ran the chop through and put it down on a ledge.

He levered the grille off the fireplace with his foot. He spat on his fingers, picked up the chop, chewed the fat off it and stared into the coals.

An ornate citadel, in which were many golden chambers, with corridors and staircases of copper and brass, and silver and lead, and bronze and pewter and aluminium foil, and other metals too numerous to mention, took shape in the heart of the fire, endured, and crumbled away.

The pockets of Mr's trousers yielded up a screw, a one cent piece, a receipt from the Buccaneer Steakhouse (1 × Dagwood, 1 × Chps, 1 × Gngr Beer), a soiled serviette, a fatty deposit slip from the United Building Society, a shirt button, a length of twine and a toothpick chewed at one end. Mrs stuffed the trousers into the washing-machine, jabbed a button to start the cycle and carried her finds to the lounge, where she arranged them on the coffee-table. She examined each of them in turn, as if each had a story to tell.

This exercise gave her an appetite for conversation. She went to her prize knick-knack cabinet and surveyed the exhibits. Budgie. Paper nautilus. Plastic troll. Worry-beads. Dinner-bell.

In the end it was a glass paperweight with a guineafowl feather aflutter in its heart that spoke to her.

Nieuwenhuizen was overcome by a great weariness. It drifted like spume from the tireless billows of veld and infiltrated the wide-open portals of his eyes, filling him slowly to the brim. His head listed, and the weariness slopped over and spilled down his cheeks. Mr Malgas advanced towards him through the rainbowed mist, parting the grass with his muscular thighs, extending his right hand like a shifting-spanner and saying, "How do you do?"

"He was sitting there like a lump all day," Mrs told Mr when he came in from work. "He was looking at our house as if there's something wrong with it."

"You shouldn't take it personally," said Mr. "He's probably just tired from his journey."

"What journey?" she demanded suspiciously. "Where did you get that?"

"I'm just supposing."

"It's not like you to suppose."

"He must have come from somewhere. He didn't sprout there like a bean."

"Ha ha, that's the spirit. Don't worry about me. I'll get used to being a prisoner in my own home."

"What can a man do?"

"A man can find out what he wants. Go over there and ask him."

Mr shrugged.

"He'd have to say something, if you asked. He couldn't just sit there with a mouth full of teeth."

Mr Malgas paused on the verge, in the twilight, to look over the plot. A thin melody mixed with the smell of cooked meat washed over him. He wasn't sure what to do next: there was no gate to rattle, no doorbell to ring. After a while something came to him, a phrase he had heard in a film about the Wild West, and he tried it out: "Hail the camp!"

The singing ceased. Nieuwenhuizen loomed in the distance, wreathed in smoke, as tall as a tree struck by lightning. Mr Malgas was tempted to run away. But one twisted branch beckoned and the human gesture heartened him. He set out across the veld.

Nieuwenhuizen looked down on his settlement from the vantage-point of the oil drum. It was a dirty mess. He thought about tidying up, stirring the coals to enhance the atmosphere, even throwing on a log, but there wasn't time. Mr Malgas drew near, breaking noisily through the undergrowth. Nieuwenhuizen stuck out his hand and grasped the cold air experimentally. Firm but friendly.

When he reached the outskirts of the camp, where the grass had been trampled flat, Mr Malgas was relieved to see that the stranger owed at least some of his height to the fact that he was standing on something. As Mr Malgas broke into the pale ring of lamplight he leapt down and came forward with his hand raised. "Hail yourself, neighbour! I've been expecting you."

"Malgas," said Mr Malgas, fixing his eyes so earnestly on the gaunt face that its features blurred, and enclosing a thorny hand in his own. It weighed next to nothing and it pricked his palm.

"Father," said the stranger.

"Pardon?"

"Father. Pleased to meet you."

"Malgas," Mr Malgas repeated slowly. "Did you say 'Father'?"

"It's odd, isn't it? Everyone says so."

"I've never come across it before." Mr Malgas sneaked a glance at the fireplace, where a blackened pot was squatting over the coals. "It seems improbable, if you don't mind me saying so."

"Be my guest. I'm used to it. And you'll get used to it too, believe me. People will get used to anything."

In the silence that followed, Nieuwenhuizen noted Malgas's Hush Puppies and his long socks bristling with blackjacks, his hairy, bulbous thighs, and a belly he tried to conceal, like a stolen melon, under the elasticized band of his shorts. Mr Malgas, while he watched Nieuwenhuizen watching him, heard the pot pass a wind and smelt singed hair, leaves, burning rubber and incense.

"Are you a priest?"

"Heavens no."

The silence sizzled.

"Pull up a stone," said Nieuwenhuizen, suddenly jovial. "Take the weight off your feet." He dragged his drum to the fireside, seated himself on it, gave his visitor a toothy grin and stirred the pot vigorously with a stick.

Mr Malgas sat on the proffered stone, with his knees sticking up like anthills and his hands hanging down between them like spades, looking at Nieuwenhuizen's unlikely limbs and listening to the pot as it bubbled and squeaked.

Nieuwenhuizen said nothing, so Mr Malgas cleared his throat and said too loudly, "I'll come straight to the point: Why are you here?"

"I'm building a new house," said Nieuwenhuizen.

Mr Malgas looked over his shoulder.

"I haven't actually started yet," said Nieuwenhuizen with a crackly laugh. "It's still in the planning stages."

"You're a builder then. I'm in hardware myself." Mr Malgas wished he had a business card to present, but he hadn't thought to bring his wallet. He was wearing a Mr Hardware T-shirt under his track-suit top, as always, but showing that would surely be improper. So he made the following conversation instead: "What brings you to our part of the world?"

"It's a long story. Have you eaten?"

"No thanks."

Nieuwenhuizen wiped his stirrer meticulously on the rim of the pot and laid it on a ledge made for that purpose. Mr Malgas saw from the protuberances at either end that what he had taken for a stick was in fact a bone. While he was inspecting it surreptitiously in an effort to determine its ancestry, Nieuwenhuizen took up a jagged bottle-neck and ladled some of his stew into a tin, plucked a plastic fork from his instep and began to eat.

"Where do you hail from?" asked Mr Malgas, rousing himself from his reverie.

"To cut a long story short: I left my home far away and came here to start over. It was a comfortable old place, give it its due, with one and a half bathrooms, but it had served its time. It was falling apart, to tell the truth. Full of maggots and tripe. The stuffing was coming out of the sofa, for example, the pipes leaked, the boards under the bath were green. I could see myself falling through them tub and all, up to my neck in hot water. The earth around there was quite rotten, and soft, a bit like cheese. I'd sink through it one day – that was my nightmare – I'd keep on going down to the centre of the planet, which is molten I'm told. Sss! Gone up in steam like a gob in a frying-pan. Can you imagine?"

Mr Malgas examined the soles of Nieuwenhuizen's boots, which were stretched out towards the heat. The rubber bore a mysterious pattern of crosses and arrows. He also looked at Nieuwenhuizen's oversized head, which bobbed constantly as if to keep its balance on his stalk of a neck; the proportions of this head no longer reassured him.

"Excuse me?"

"Are you sure you won't have a little something?" Nieuwenhuizen repeated, pointing to the pot and smacking his lips. He observed with approval the inquisitive look on his guest's face.

"That reminds me: I must be getting back."

"You've just arrived." Nieuwenhuizen lifted a leaf-green mass on the end of his fork and blew on it. He turned his eyes on Malgas's face, noting that the putty-coloured cheeks were now tinged with a rare shade of pink, and then allowed his attention to wander, over his guest's beefy shoulder, to the wall, with its unsettling combination of wagon-wheels and suns. "Now that I've got you here, perhaps you can clear up a little question for me. That wall of yours, with the suns – are they rising or setting?"

Mr Malgas stood up very slowly, as if his belly weighed too much, and gazed across the desolate savannah. The light from his lounge window glowed comfortingly in the wedges between spokes and rays. No matter how hard he looked at them, the suns didn't budge – but he did notice a curtain twitching. Now he remembered building the wall. Mrs said, "Wheels and suns in one wall? What will people think?" And he explained about discontinued lines, the principle of odds and ends, and discounts that were never to be repeated. It was simple. But rising or setting? Who could have foreseen such a poser? He sat down again. Nieuwenhuizen's eyes were shining.

"I must be going now. Mrs will be wondering what's become of me."

Nieuwenhuizen raised his shoulders in a resigned shrug and said, "You must drop in again, and bring the Mrs with you. I must say I've enjoyed exchanging words with you. It passed the time very pleasantly."

Mr Malgas pushed back his stone. He felt compelled to say: "If you need anything – bricks, cement, timber, you name it – just yell. Mr Hardware, Helpmekaar Centre. I'm in the Yellow Pages."

"That's kind of you, thanks. Good night then, Malgas."

"Good night . . . Father."

Mr Malgas walked purposefully away. "Fancy me calling him 'Father'," he thought, "he's my age if he's a day."

Mr Hardware, Nieuwenhuizen thought as Malgas disappeared from sight. Blow me down.

Through a crack in the curtains Mrs watched Mr tiptoeing towards the camp, as if he was afraid of making a sound, and bowing into the light. He sat awkwardly on a stone, like a scolded child. His behaviour embarrassed her and she blushed, alone as she was, and turned away.

Quickly, in order of appearance: Doily. Dust-cover. Double boiler. Decanter. Doom. *Découpage.* Dicky-bird.

The incantation failed: she could not keep her distance. She returned to the window and was just in time to watch Mr bowing out of the light and blundering back the way he had come, or rather, the way he had *gone,* looking fearfully around him as if he was afraid of the dark.

In alphabetical order then, slowly: Decanter. *Découpage.* Dicky-bird. Hum.

"If you ask me, he's in real estate," Mr said. "Property development, renovations, restorations, upgrading, that sort of thing."

"I ask you," Mrs said archly and crooked one tatty eyebrow into a question mark.

"A jack of all trades, but retired now and living off the proceeds. He didn't say it in so many words, mind, I'm making deductions, so don't quote me."

"That doesn't answer my question. What does he want?"

"He doesn't *want* anything. He's building a house."

"A house?"

"A new one. Probably a double-storey."

"A double-storey? Bang goes our privacy!"

"Never mind that. In this day and age it's security that counts. You can't afford to have an empty plot on your doorstep. Ask anyone. It attracts the wrong elements."

"Building operations, I can just see it, noise and nuisance, generators, compressors, pneumatic hammers, concrete-mixers going day and night, strange men – builders. Dust all over my ornaments. It's terrible. I'll complain."

"It'll all be worth it in the end. He's going to put up a mansion here, if I know him, a magnificent place. Raise the tone of the neighbour-hood, not to mention the property values. There may even be a bit of business in it for us."

"Count me out. You can deal with him all on your own."

Mrs turned up the volume. The minimum and maximum tempera-tures forecast for the following day by the Weather Bureau scrolled solemnly upwards against a backdrop of violins and autumn leaves. Mrs inhaled noisily through her teeth, drew her cardigan around her shoulders and turned the sound down again.

"I never should have bricked up the fireplace," Mr said. "It would be homely to sit around the hearth with one's feet propped on the fender."

"And then where would we put the TV?"

They both looked at the set, which stood on a trolley on the old hearthstone. A man spoke silently to them, they could tell he was speaking by the movement of his moustache. Then the economic indi-cators appeared against a backdrop of trumpets (which they could not hear) and paper money.

"So what was he doing with himself? I don't suppose he was watch-ing television, like a normal human being."

"He was cooking his dinner, actually, in one of those two-legged pots."

"Come again."

"In one of those pots with legs, you know the ones I mean."

"I heard that. You know as well as I do those pots have three legs."

"I know," said Mr with feeling, "but this one looked for all the world as if it had *two*."

"Are you nuts?"

"The third was obscured, no doubt."

"Of course it was. How could a pot stand up on two legs?"

"True."

"So what was in this pot?"

"God knows. He offered me some, he was very hospitable, but with dinner waiting for me here at home, I naturally declined."

"I'd give my right arm to know what was in that pot . . ."

"It was some sort of stew. It didn't smell too bad either, out in the open, under the stars. Fresh air always gives me an appetite."

"Probably some poor domestic animal."

They both watched an advertisement for life insurance, which they knew by heart even without the sound. It was about facing up to death.

"I wasn't going to mention it, it's not important, but he asked me the strangest question, with a straight face too. You know the wall? You know the wagon-wheels?" Mrs prepared a triumphant expression but Mr cut her short with, "Well, not them. You know the suns? . . . He wanted to know whether they were rising or setting."

"Now I've heard everything," said Mrs. "Any fool can see that they're setting."

Nieuwenhuizen emptied the remains of his stew into a gourd, sealed its neck with a wad of masticated wax-paper, slipped it into a cradle made from a wire coat-hanger and hung it on a branch of the tree beyond the claws of nocturnal scavengers. He scraped the burnt rind from the inside of the pot into the coals, where it produced a lot of acrid smoke, filled the pot with water and left it to soak. Then he unpacked a leather bandoleer and a tin of dubbin from the portmanteau and set to work.

"Mrs! . . . I said, Mrs!"
    "Ja."

There was whittling to be done, there was twisting, there was hammering, and of course there was drowsing. When he was not pottering on his property, learning the lie of the land, Nieuwenhuizen sat under his tree, keeping his hands busy and nodding off.

Mrs Malgas observed all his doings, secretly at first, and then more openly as it became apparent that her presence made no impression on him. She took to perching on a stool behind the net curtain in the lounge, knitting, flipping through a magazine, turning questions about his motives over in her mind as if they were cards. She didn't like him. Specifically, she didn't like the way he jiggled his head and the way he hitched up his pants with his thumbs, which he stuck into his pockets, fanning out his fingers as if he didn't want to dirty the cloth. She didn't like his jaunty gait and his drifting off and staring into space. More generally, she didn't like to think that he had come for no other purpose than to upset her and turn things upside-down. She didn't like to think about him at all.

So she distracted herself by making inventories of her knick-knacks: copper ashtray, Weltevreden coat of arms (wildebeest rampant). Wicker basket, yellow, a-tisket. Figurines, viz. cobbler, gypsy, ballerina, plumber, horologist, Smurf. Paperweight, guineafowl feather. Paperweight, rose. Paperweight, Merry Pebbles Holiday Chalets. Cake-lifter, Continental China, coronation centenary crockery, crenate, crumbs. However. Spatula. Just as things were starting to become interesting. Mug. As day followed day. Doll. As day follows night. Puppy-dog. As night follows day, sure enough, she found herself drawn back to the window.

Nieuwenhuizen's wanderings over the veld, as much as they annoyed her, reassured her too by their aimlessness. They made him seem indecisive, ineffectual and itinerant. But when he settled down under the tree to hammer beer tins into soup-plates, to tinker with fragments of pottery and polystyrene, to plait ribbons of plastic into ropes, to carve and whittle and twist, to hammer holes through and bind together, it seemed that he was practising for something bigger, it became conceivable that he really would build a house next door, a house in the contemporary style made entirely of recycled material, a disposable, three-bedroomed family home held together by the dowels of his own ramshackle purpose, and that he would occupy it, permanently – and this prospect made her feel utterly despondent.

"We have to be realistic about this," Mrs said to Mr on a Friday evening when the conversation turned inevitably to Nieuwenhuizen. "We have to act like responsible adults and stop thinking about ourselves alone. He's dangerous. Ask yourself: Where does he go? Does he dig a hole and squat over it like a dog?"

"A cat," said Mr irritably.

"I'm talking about the principle. Where does he get his water from? He's got a drumful there, for washing and cooking and all his household needs. Probably siphons it out of our pool in the dead of night, when normal people are sleeping."

"We could offer to supply him with a drop of water. We've got plenty. I could run a hose over to his place easily enough."

"What does he eat? What's cooking in that two-legged pot of his? Four-legged chickens? Pigeons? Cockatoos and budgerigars?"

"There's another neighbourly thing we could do – if you didn't dislike him so: we could give him a square meal from time to time."

"Where does he get his money? He's got money, surely?"

"Sigh!"

"How many times must I ask you not to say that? You know how much it annoys me!"

"It's just an expression."

"Why can't you sigh like everybody else? How would you like it if I said 'Laugh' all the time instead of laughing?"

Mr thought about that as he slipped out into the garden. Only the night before he had chanced upon a picturesque view of Nieuwenhuizen's camp, framed between two spokes of a wagon-wheel, and he was anxious to recapture it; with luck he would pick up a wholesome aroma and a snatch of some melody or other. A welcome breeze stirred a ripple of applause in the shrubbery. He smelt chlorine, creosote and mint. The swimming-pool's Kreepy Krauly was silent, asleep in the depths below the diving-board, but the water echoed the slapping of his sandals against the soles of his feet as he made his way to the side of the house, along a Slasto pathway he had laid himself.

Mash through strainer da-da-da. Return pulp to stove, bring back to boil and simmer for 30 mins. Add seasoning.

Mrs Malgas shook Mixed Herbs into her palm and tipped them into the pot. She pinched salt and pepper, she dashed Tabasco, she squeezed lemon. She stirred and tasted. Bland. She spiked the mixture with a handful of cloves as piquant as upholstery tacks.

As the days had passed Mr Malgas had developed a conviction, which his wife was well aware of although he had not chosen to share it with her, that he was connected in some important way to Nieuwenhuizen – "Father," as he named him to himself with difficulty. They had not spoken since their first meeting, which Mr Malgas rehearsed constantly in his mind, but when he left for work in the mornings and when he returned home in the evenings he would give a few cheerful blasts on his hooter and Nieuwenhuizen would invariably pop up somewhere on the plot and respond with a wave. Such simple reciprocal gestures struck Mr Malgas as a form of co-operation with his new neighbour, foreshadowing a more meaningful relationship, which presented itself as a series of words all starting with "c," each one a node on a scale of intimacy: collaboration, coexistence, collusion.

Yet the distance which now prevailed between them, a distance familiarity was bound to bridge, seemed necessary, even desirable.

Concealed behind his ambiguous wall on this unprepossessing evening, with the breeze bearing the woody tang of the great outdoors to his nostrils, Mr Malgas was shaken by a thrill of suppressed excitement the likes of which he had not experienced since he was a boy playing hide-and-seek.

Nieuwenhuizen's head quivered, as if Mr Malgas's greedy gaze had joggled it, and seemed about to swivel in his direction.

But a bowl of brazen light dropped suddenly over Mr as he knelt in the shadow of the wall. Mrs had slammed the curtains open like two sheets of metal and stood in the garish window-frame brandishing a serving-spoon and looking down on him disdainfully.

"You're making a fool of us," she said while he was dusting the sand off his knees on the back step. "He pitches up out of nowhere and you, of all people, welcome him with open arms. You should be ashamed of yourself. We don't have a clue who he is. He has no history. Are you listening to me? We don't even know his name."

"We know that," said Mr, brushing past her and sagging down at the kitchen table. He watched her mangy slippers twitching impatiently. "He told me, when I was over there last week. Why don't you dish, it's getting cold."

"You didn't say anything."

"I was going to."

"Well?"

"It's 'Father'."

. . .

– 44 –

"Father?"

One thing leads to another. Nieuwenhuizen, rolling on the ground, yelping in agony, clasping his left hand between his knees, cursing himself, landed up in the remains of the cooking-fire. Just moments before, he had brought his hammer down on his thumb-nail. That opposable pain was forgotten now as he tossed and turned to shake off the clinging coals. The hair on his head crackled, budded into flame, bloomed – but he crushed the petals with an oily chamois. When the crisis was over he composed himself once again in front of his tent, sucking his thumb and nursing his blistered elbow, and through his tears, which were two parts pain and one part embarrassment, saw Malgas on the horizon.

Mr Malgas found the approach to the camp more welcoming this time: a teetering fence-post, emitting a tang of fresh creosote and surmounted by a scuffed cement shoe with a little stable-door, two sash-windows and a slot in its toe-cap, marked the beginning of a path through the veld, and he took it gratefully. Several twists and turns dictated by the geography brought him to an anthill, where he rested and enjoyed the prospect. Then he went on, in two minds about whether to announce his arrival.

Nieuwenhuizen saw Malgas coming down the path fending off spider's webs with his hands and hacking away at lianas with a rusty panga, and in the event it was he who called out a greeting. "Malgas!"

Nieuwenhuizen was sitting in the mouth of his tent, on the untidy pile of his own long legs, busy with some handiwork concealed in his lap.

"Hello Father!" Malgas was pleased at how naturally the name flew from his lips. If Nieuwenhuizen was also pleased he did not show it, but merely waved a pair of pliers in the direction of a stone and went on with his work.

"This is coming along nicely," said Malgas, turning in an appreciative circle. "Mind if I look around?"

Taking a shrug as permission, Mr Malgas made a tour of the camp and its environs, allowing the rudimentary footpaths that had appeared with time to guide his steps. He took a childlike delight in the signs he found everywhere that the plot had become lived in, that the newcomer had made himself at home. "A dwelling-place *carved out of the veld*," Malgas thought happily, examining the bare, compacted soil around the hearth. A soothing smell rising up from below notified him that the earth had been sprinkled with water to settle the dust.

"Where the hell is my hammer?" Nieuwenhuizen asked himself.

Malgas hunted obligingly for a hammer at the foot of the tree, and discovered instead a pile of firewood and fence-posts, which he took to be the raw materials of fortifications that had yet to be constructed; next to that was a leather portmanteau, sturdily made but a little the worse for wear, probably imitation, plastered with name-tags, illegible, every one of them, and stickers – exotic destinations: Bordeaux, Florida, Eldorado Park – and spilling various items of clothing; then a metal drum, lipping with green water, and a tin ladle displaying in its bowl the label of a popular soft drink. On an impulse he scooped a ladleful of water and poured it over his head, and although there was a nip in the air and he was required to suppress the lip-smacking, hair-tossing display of pleasure he associated with the gesture, he nevertheless felt invigorated.

"Here it is!" Nieuwenhuizen said. "I've been sitting on it all along."

Malgas circumnavigated the tree and the tent, noting with approval the prudent depth of the moat and testing the tension of the guy-ropes. Some bulky objects hung in plastic bags from the lower branches of the tree. Malgas, who prided himself on his knowledge of packaging and its relationship to contents, could not resist the challenge. After an inquiring glance at the back of Nieuwenhuizen's grizzled head he palpated one of the bags thoroughly, but to his surprise could not determine what it contained. Never mind, he moved on. Behind the tent he found some implements that were more readily identifiable: a row of rough-hewn wooden spoons dangling from a length of string (the stirring-bone was nowhere to be seen), a stack of misshapen plates and saucers, a tin of creosote with a brush resting across it, a hurricane-lamp, a slab of discoloured slate supporting a grey liver. He prodded this dismal organ with a blunt forefinger and found it firm. But in a cove under the hedge were yet other gadgets whose functions he could not divine, despite his many years of experience in Hardware.

"You've got some fascinating things here," Malgas exclaimed. "What's this?" He held up a contraption consisting of a luminous orange traffic-beacon mounted upside-down in a cardboard box and bound with copper wire.

Nieuwenhuizen's head spun round. He looked at the eager expression on Malgas's face and at his thick fingers gripping the gadget. "Bush rain-gauge," he said sadly, "calibrated, measures rainfall. Horn also works."

"Useful . . . And this?"

"Mousetrap. Field-mice."

"This?"

"Cookie cutter."

Nieuwenhuizen found the questions tiresome.

"What's that you're making there?" Malgas asked, though he was not insensitive to Nieuwenhuizen's tone. As he spoke he rolled a stone closer and sat down on it. He was disappointed to find that Nieuwenhuizen's torso blocked his view of the tent's interior.

"This is a teacup," said Nieuwenhuizen, holding up a dented tin and turning it from side to side so that Malgas could admire it. "Almost finished. Just got to round off the handle here." He perked up suddenly, shooting out one leg like a railway signal. "Let's make a pot of tea and you may have the honour of testing out my cup."

The coals in the fireplace were warm. Under Nieuwenhuizen's attentive gaze, Malgas fetched kindling from the woodpile, built up a fire, ladled water into the pot, noting with relief that it had three legs after all, and, following instructions, measured the requisite quantity of dried leaves from a plastic bag. "What is this stuff?" he asked as he sprinkled the leaves onto the bubbling water.

"Herbaceous infusion," Nieuwenhuizen replied. "Tisane, excuse the jargon. Very good for you. Purifies the blood and builds you up."

When the tea had steeped to Nieuwenhuizen's satisfaction, Malgas was instructed to strain it through a shop-soiled oil-filter and sweeten it with honey from a jar.

Malgas reported that the new teacup served its purpose adequately – it certainly didn't leak – but its serrated rim threatened his lip and its ear was too small to accommodate his forefinger.

"I'm afraid it's made for a less substantial digit," Nieuwenhuizen explained with a good-humoured cackle, holding up his own skinny forefinger to illustrate the point. "Oh my."

Despite the honey the tea tasted of oil and rust.

"This is the life," said Malgas, when they were both ensconced on stones with their teacups resting on their stomachs and their legs stretched out to catch the afternoon sun.

A silty silence descended upon them. Malgas savoured its meaningful elements: the rubbery squeaking of his host's boots against a grease-spattered stone; the hissing of the sticks in the fireplace; insects scurrying in the grass; dry leaves rattling in the hedge; his cup hiccuping as its joints expanded; a distant roar of traffic.

Through half-closed lids Nieuwenhuizen charted the outstanding features of Malgas's face, ear to ear and quiff to chin.

When they had drained their cups, Malgas sighed contentedly and said, "So. When does the building begin?"

"Patience, patience," Nieuwenhuizen murmured sleepily, screwing his eyes shut to make Malgas disappear. "I've got all the time in the world." The breathless pause that followed insisted that further explanation was called for. "You can't rush the building of a new house.

You've got to get the whole thing clear in the mind's eye." Another pause insisted. "Take it from me. I've been acclimatizing, building up my strength for the first phase: namely, the clearing of the virgin bushveld."

"What do you consume, to build yourself up I mean?"

"Oh, birds, roots, that kind of thing. Berries. I'm living off the land. Naturally, I get my basics from the corner café, and the occasional luxury to keep me going. I'm especially fond of a chocolate digestive."

The air thickened. Nieuwenhuizen kept his eyes closed. Minutes coalesced into hours, oozed by, and Malgas found himself dozing off. Perhaps it was the tea? Or was it Nieuwenhuizen's husky voice, rising and falling like a wind through the treetop?

They discussed edible ground cover, drifted off, moulds, hydroponics, broccoli, market gardens, touched on barter (Nieuwenhuizen waved a bath mat woven from plastic bags), drifted off again, bumped against Hardware (Malgas revealed his T-shirt, which showed an overalled manikin, who bore a passing resemblance to Malgas himself, holding a huge spangled nail in one hand and a hammer in the other), hinges, handles, hafts, wallpaper, sandpaper, zinc, sink, sank, surfaced again into the niceties of skinning a cat, dropped off, slid in slow motion through spec housing and restaurant rubbish bins, recycled waste and domestic security gates, found themselves talking about the weather.

At length the sun dipped towards the red roof of Malgas's house, which for some time had appeared to him through his eyelashes as a distant koppie. Then the elongated shadow of his wall touched his toes and he awoke to an uncomfortable recollection of the purpose of his visit.

"You find out what his real name is," Mrs Malgas had announced bitterly, "or don't even bother to come back."

Mr Malgas looked into the swampy bottom of his teacup and assembled a question.

The house, when it was emptied of Mr's absorbing presence, seemed more full of objects. They multiplied and grew in stature, their edges became sharper, their surfaces more reflective. Mrs Malgas moved among them, running a finger along the scalloped edges of display cabinets, stooping to blow dust off polished table-tops, pinching fluff off the velveteen shoulders of armchairs. She felt lonely. Mr had been gone for hours, and she could no longer bear the sight of him, reclining at the fireside with his hands behind his head and his feet up, as if he was in the privacy of his own home.

She took a bone-china shoe from the mantelpiece and turned it over in her hands. The shoe was slim and white, with a gilt buckle and a wineglass heel. It feels as if I've always had this, she thought, but that's impossible. Always. Slipper. It must have come from somewhere? A gift from Mr? For some reason, it called to mind the day on which he'd bricked up the fireplace. She saw him, kneeling in front of the gaping hole, holding a trowel laden with wet cement in one hand and a brick in the other. His hair was standing on end and his shoulders were dandruffed with plaster chips and wood shavings. When she came in with the tea-tray he looked over one flaky shoulder and smiled woodenly, as if he was an advertisement for DIY products.

Suddenly the air was infused with the smell of meat. Mrs Malgas turned to the TV set on the hearth. A pitchfork hoisted a slab of red meat the size of a doorstep and threw it down on a grille. A familiar anthem, all sticky-fingered strings and saucy brass, came to the boil as the meat rebounded in slow motion from the grille, splashing large drops of fat and marinade. The smell of meat, basted in the surging melody, was overpowering. Mrs Malgas shut her eyes and fumbled for the flames, she felt the hot screen against her palms, a tacky button, she pressed it. She swallowed her nausea and held the cool sole of the shoe to her burning cheek.

The set was still sizzling when Mr Malgas traipsed in and switched on the light. The startled planes of the room banged into one another and fell back into their accustomed order.

Mr sat down on his La-Z-Boy with his hands dangling.

Mrs looked at the damp shadows on his shirt. "You're a sight for sore eyes," she said.

"What's been going on now?" He looked at the blank screen.

"Nothing."

She put the china shoe back in its place. The TV set felt warm against her belly. She said, "So."

He cleaned one fingernail with another.

"You did ask him?"

"I did. 'Father' turns out to be a nickname of sorts."

She raised an eyebrow.

"As luck would have it, his real name is 'Nieuwenhuizen'."

The name snapped in half in the air and the two pieces dropped like twigs into the shaggy carpet. Mr hunted for them under the pretext of tying his shoelaces until her shadow fell over him.

"That's impossible," she said. "It's too much of a coincidence."

Mr looked at her slippers. The sheepskin was the same colour as the carpet. He saw her glossy shins, sprouting from the bulbs of her feet like saplings, and his own hands burrowing in the tufted fibres as if he was trying to uproot her. The idea made him uncomfortable. He raised his eyes to her face. It was scrunched into a small, livid fruit. In the juicy pulp of the eyes the pupils glinted like pips.

"I ask you," she said, hawking. "Nieuwenhuizen of all things." Her tongue held the two parts of the name together precisely, as if she was waiting for the glue to dry. "Nieuwenhuizen! Obviously an alias. A stage name. Did you ask for ID?"

"Nieuwenhuizen is a common name," he said, focusing on her mouth.

"A criminal," the mouth said. "I knew it. A killer."

"I was at school with one."

"Please," said Mrs, using an intonation she had acquired from American television programmes, as Mr walked out of the room with his laces dragging behind him like dropped reins.

"Please," she said again, as he returned in his socks, carrying the telephone directory. He flung the directory open on the coffee-table and rummaged through it. "Here: Nieuwenhuizen, C. J. of Roosevelt

Park. A midwife, it says. Nieuwenhuizen, D. L. of Malvern East, just down the road. Nieuwenhuizen, H. A. of Pine Park. Another Nieuwenhuizen, H. A. of Rndprkrf. Where's that?"

Mrs knew, but she didn't feel like telling.

"Never mind." His finger cut a furrow down the page. "There must be twenty of them, thirty if you count the Nieuwhuises and the Nieuwhuyses and the Niehauses. There's probably a Newhouse too." He flipped. "What have we here? No. But there's a Newburg, and a list of Newmans as long as my arm."

"We live in the west," she said, going over to the window, "but our name isn't Van der Westhuizen."

"That's my argument exactly! We may not be called Van der Westhuizen – I'll grant you that – but thousands of people are, at least, say, what . . . five thousand? . . . and many of them *are* to the west of something. See?" Her shoulders drooped, and he went on triumphantly, "There must be thousands of Nieuwenhuizens countrywide, and at any given moment I'll bet a dozen of them are building new houses – or thinking about it, anyway. It's the luck of the draw. No, that's feeble. It's the law of averages."

"It's too good to be true."

Mr Malgas went to stand beside his wife. Nieuwenhuizen had built up the fire and was walking slowly round it, dragging his long shadow over the landscape.

After a while of looking straight through it, Mr Malgas became aware of his own face reflected in the glass. Then he saw that his whole body was there, floating in the chilly space beyond the burglar-bars, and his wife's face too, with its body below, and their lounge and its familiar clutter, dangerously cantilevered, and Nieuwenhuizen's fire blazing in the middle of the carpet where the coffee-table should be. Tenderly, Mr put his arm around Mrs's shoulders and drew her to him, and watched his pale reflection in the other room mimic the gesture.

"You shouldn't hate him," he said, "and there's no need to be afraid of him. Even if it turns out that he's not who he says he is, and I'm not saying it will, he means no harm. Look at him, out there in the cold, while we're here in our cosy home. I almost feel sorry for him – although that's unnecessary, as he'd be quick to point out. He's very resourceful. He's got a tea-set made out of tins and everything."

She shrugged her shoulders under his heavy arm. "It can only bring trouble . . . and insects," she whispered. After a pause, during which Mr listened intently to the silence of the house but could discern no sign of life, she said firmly, "Go ahead and be his friend. You'll do as you please anyway, I know. But don't come crying to me when he lets you down. And don't expect me to call him 'Nieuwenhuizen'. It's even worse than 'Father'. If I have to refer to him at all, I'll just say 'Him', and you'll know why."

What is it with this Malgas? Nieuwenhuizen asked himself. He seems eager to serve. But he's full of questions, and so hard to convince.

Nieuwenhuizen! he'd exclaimed. Really? Are you serious?

For Pete's sake.

The more persuasively Nieuwenhuizen laid claim to the word that was his name, the more detached he felt from it. It was a distressing experience, watching his personal noun drift away on the air.

But people will get used to almost anything.

By a circuitous process of reasoning, during which he walked round and round his fire until he was quite dizzy, Nieuwenhuizen reattached his name and decided that Malgas should be kept guessing.

The left foot of Mrs, which was daintily arched and pigeon-toed, stepped out of the bath, dripping soapy water, and stretched down to the floor, where it met with something cold and slimy. A plastic bath mat. She knew at once whose hideous creation it was.

Although she was loath to touch this gewgaw, she wanted to know more about it, as if that would teach her something important about Him.

She lifted the mat with the end of Mr's toothbrush. Chkrs. It was woven, no, one really couldn't call it weaving. It was knitted, knotted, out of plastic shopping bags. She identified three major supermarket chains by the predominance of certain colours and fragments of lettering. Pick n Pay. There seemed to be a Mr Hardware packet in there somewhere, sandy lettering on a muddy ground, but she couldn't be sure. The words were warped into the fabric of the thing and could not be unravelled.

She dropped the mat in the bin under the hand-wash basin and sat on the toilet seat, wrapped in her towel, trying to figure out when Mr had smuggled it into her house. He was becoming more devious by the day.

The next morning Nieuwenhuizen hailed Mr Malgas as he went out to buy the Sunday newspapers and hurried over to meet him on the verge. "Phase One is upon us, Malgas," he said earnestly. "Last night, after our little man to man, I got to thinking about the future I asked myself the question: 'Is it time?' And the answer came back, loud and clear, in a tell-tale itching of the palms of the hands and the soles of the feet: 'You can bet your boots it is.'"

"To do what?"

"I was coming to that: To 'clear the land'!" He threw his hands up in two V signs and scored quotation marks around the words with his fingernails. "May I borrow a spade?"

"Only with pleasure!"

Malgas was delighted that the action was about to begin at last. He was also secretly touched that Nieuwenhuizen had said "upon *us*" rather than "upon me." He fetched a spade from his garage and gave expert instructions about its use. Then he rushed off to the café, promising to return in two ticks.

Nieuwenhuizen ran a finger over the blade. It was blunt. He began sharpening it on a kerbstone. Before long he heard Malgas huffing and puffing back, and he quickly retired to the inner reaches of the plot (block IVF) and threw himself into his task.

Malgas was not so easily put off. He craned his neck. "Need a hand there Father?"

"Thanks but no thanks," Nieuwenhuizen responded without looking up. "I'll give you a call when I need you. You go home and catch up on the news."

Malgas went sadly on his way.

Nieuwenhuizen set upon the vegetation with a vengeance, flattening stems with his boots and hacking at roots with his spade. In a minute he was immersed in a cloud of dust and scented sap, which he gulped down in dry, foaming draughts. The brew was intoxicating.

Mr Malgas watched the slaughter from his lounge, and then from his kitchen, and finally, as the dust thickened, from the side of his house through the garden wall. He found Nieuwenhuizen's methods outlandish. The man wielded the spade with authority despite his off-beat sense of rhythm, and he had stamina, you had to admit. There was power in his thin arms too, for with one blow he was capable of shearing a small shrub clean off at the root, leaving nothing but a cross-section of stem like a peppermint spat out in the dust.

But his technique . . . What could one say? It was flawed. He spent an inordinate amount of energy on purely decorative effects. Between blows he liked to hum a bar or two from a march and lay about him with the spade, inscribing fleeting arabesques and curlicues on the moted air. He also enjoyed twirling it like a baton, whirling it like an umbrella and tossing it up like a drum-major's mace. In a different context these affectations might have served to demonstrate his dexterity, but strange to say here they had the opposite effect: the implement, moving gracefully through space, acquired a life of its own. Rather than guiding it, Nieuwenhuizen seemed to trip after it like a clumsy dancing partner, flinging his limbs in many directions.

"The worst thing about all this tomfoolery," Mr Malgas thought, "is the amount of precious time it wastes."

Nieuwenhuizen was unstoppable. When a tap-root resisted his assault he hopped up on the spade with his boots on either side of the handle and swayed backwards and forwards like a jockey, driving the blade underground. Then he threw his weight upon the handle and popped a sod as big as his head out of the earth.

Day after day, block by labelled block, the deforestation went on. The call for Mr Malgas never came. But he was not one to stand on ceremony: every evening after work he went next door uninvited, bearing some little excuse for a visit filched from the store. On Monday, for example, it was a brand-new spade with a pillar-box red ferrule to match Nieuwenhuizen's tent; on Tuesday, again, it was a pitchfork to match the spade and a five-litre keg of fuel for the hurricane-lamp.

Nieuwenhuizen humoured him.

.   .   .

Wednesday's defoliation brought Nieuwenhuizen something out of the ordinary. At noon he was cutting a wide swath through a thicket of kakiebos when he came across his anthill. This scenic attraction had been missing without trace for several days and it gave him quite a turn to bump into it in the middle of nowhere. He composed himself by stropping his new blade unnecessarily on the Malgases' wall.

Nieuwenhuizen had always assumed, without giving the matter much thought, that the anthill was full of ants. (By "always," of course, he meant since his arrival on the plot.) He imagined the demolition of the hill: his blade would find lubricated grooves in the air to slot into, it would swoop with a whistle and cleave through the crown with a corky pop. Then wave upon wave of hot red ants would boil down the slopes.

But when he tried to breach the surface his blade rebounded with a hand-numbing clang. It took hours of patient chipping with the sharp point of the blade to break through the shell, and then he exposed nothing but an elaborate system of empty corridors. He hacked a thick chunk of the stuff from the core, which was softer than the shell and riddled with holes like a Swiss cheese, and examined it more closely: no sign of life.

It was too much for him. He went to bed.

When Mr Malgas arrived that evening he found Nieuwenhuizen shut up in his tent, fast asleep. The stillness of the camp was unnerving. The visitor made his offerings – a Cadac gas-bottle which he had filled with his own hands and a Mr Hardware T-shirt, XL – and went back home.

.   .   .

Mrs had the full story. She wanted to re-enact it too, with her fish-knife and a heap of creamed cauliflower, but Mr wouldn't hear of it.

"He trimmed the grass all round neatly," she insisted. "It reminded me of when you had that mole removed and Dr Dinnerstein —"

"Mr Dinnerstein," Mr corrected her. "Now stop playing with your food and eat up."

Not everyone is cut out to retail Hardware. In a day's work a hardware man might have to arrive at creative solutions to a dozen all-important little problems. Mr Malgas, who was ideally suited to the vocation, was upset to find that he couldn't concentrate. He dispensed tacks instead of panel-pins and insecticide instead of whitewash.

Insects. He couldn't get them out of his mind. Mrs was right: there had been a remarkable increase in their numbers recently.

On Thursday evening he had three excuses for visiting Nieuwenhuizen: a carton of mosquito coils, a stick of insect repellent and a length of fly-paper that he insisted on tying to a branch of the thorn-tree. On Friday, by contrast, he took a newfangled contraption which allowed one to balance a three-legged pot on top of a gas-bottle and so eliminated the bother of building a fire.

Nieuwenhuizen accepted these gifts with equanimity. He took each one in both hands, looked at it from different sides and said, "Thank you, it's just what I need." Then he found a place to stow it and looked at his benefactor expectantly.

Malgas would have appreciated a more enthusiastic response,

especially to the gas-bottle gizmo, which he thought would suit Nieuwenhuizen down to the ground. But he was satisfied all the same. Each evening he was able to inspect the building site. He was pleased to see that progress was being made, even though the grid system escaped him and he felt a pang when he saw the footpaths vanishing under swaths of cut grass and topsoil.

As he made his rounds he arranged the practical considerations of building a new house into ear-catching pairs, the easier to enumerate their pros and cons – bricks and mortar, nuts and bolts, ups and downs (in relation to pipes, this was), rands and cents, days and weeks. Nieuwenhuizen, hunkering down at the fire to stir some simmering brew or reclining before the tent gazing up at the heavens, chuckled inwardly but would not be drawn. Undeterred, Malgas always found the opportunity to say something like, "Remember now, when you get round to the actual construction as such, I'm right here on your doorstep. I'm handy. Make a note of it. Here, tie this around your finger."

Malgas was demonstrating the versatility of the new cooking gizmo on Friday night when Nieuwenhuizen butted in to take up his offer of assistance. "Why don't you come over first thing tomorrow and give me a hand to get rid of this compost."

At that moment Malgas heard a metallic click in the air between Nieuwenhuizen and himself. More than likely it was the gizmo slotting into place on the gas-bottle. But Malgas came to believe that it was his relationship with Nieuwenhuizen shifting gear from co-operation to collaboration.

.   .   .

At dawn on the appointed day Malgas shouldered a brand-new rake (the price-tag was still wrapped around one of its colour-co-ordinated teeth) and marched next door.

"Malgas."

"Father."

"How goes?"

"Well. Yourself?"

"Raring to go."

"Same here."

"Good."

They went on in this way, exhaling small talk in fussily pinked clouds of condensation, while Nieuwenhuizen decanted two mugs of coffee from the three-legged pot. Malgas was so caught up in the drama of the situation that he didn't think to ask after the gas-bottle gizmo. He found himself copying Nieuwenhuizen's clipped sentences. The restraint of the exchange marked it as a prelude to constructive effort and Malgas was proud to keep up his end.

"Sugar?"

"One."

"Honey . . ."

"Better."

They sipped the scalding coffee. "It's got a muddy aftertaste," Malgas thought. "And what's this afloat in it? Fish-scales?" But he didn't care, it was strong and stimulating. The ear of the mug still would not admit his finger, but that didn't matter either, because he preferred to curl his hands around the hot tin bowl, the way his host did.

Nieuwenhuizen put forward a plan of action, starting with the grid – big letters down this side and Roman numbers down that – and explaining tersely how one might approach the intersections as appropriate points at which to heap up the dead vegetation. Then he posed an important question: At a later stage, when the ground had been cleared in an economical fashion, might one not convey each of these small provisional heaps to a depot in the vicinity of the camp, on the spot now occupied by the fireplace, and amalgamate them into one mountain to facilitate the incineration? No?

Malgas listened with mounting excitement. The grid system was a revelation. As for the words hovering in bubbles around Nieuwenhuizen's head, moored to his lips by filaments of saliva – "economical," "provisional," "accumulation," "depot," "vicinity," "incineration" – they left him in no doubt that a great deal of intelligent forethought had gone into the plan, and he felt a thrill of vindication. With a full heart he set out for the work-station allocated to him on the wagon-wheel frontier. Nieuwenhuizen stayed behind at the tent, tinkering with one of his gadgets.

"Wish me luck, Father."

"Good luck, Malgas."

The sun was rising as usual behind the hedge when Malgas tramped across the devastated plot. Grass and weeds mown down, fractured stems and lacerated leaves, flayed boles and bulbs, dismembered trunks and dislocated roots told a moving tale of cruelty and kindness in the name of progress. The carpet underfoot was steeped in dew and its own spilt fluids, and it offered up a savoury aroma as he passed over.

The sun brushed the back of his neck with tepid fingers and made him shiver with anticipation. His eyes in turn caressed the bruised skin of the horizon, and then snagged on the protruding tip of his own rooftop. It was stained, he noticed, with the blood of the dawn. He went on bravely. The house thrust itself up through the horizon with every step he took, until it squatted clean and complete in the early morning air. The walls were as white as paper, the windows in them were blinding mirrors. The wagon-wheels began to plash through the sunshine: soon he would be bathed in the full splendour of a new working day.

Malgas arrived at the wall and took his stand. He squinted back the way he had come. For a split second he lost sight of the purpose of his journey – but before this seed of doubt could germinate, his eye fell on Nieuwenhuizen in the distance, in the lee of the hedge, with his fork pointing dramatically into the air. As if they had rehearsed this moment carefully beforehand, Malgas raised the rake in a reciprocal gesture. There was a symmetrical pause, charged with intent. Then, as one man, they set to.

Malgas spread his feet and put his head down. The shaft of the rake slid through his fist, the teeth bit into the matted stalks and stems, he drew the bounty in. At first he felt stiff and clumsy. But at each pass the rake grew more accustomed to use, as if the wood itself had softened to the shape of his hands.

Nieuwenhuizen struck up a song, but Malgas shut his ears to it, went in search of the rhythm in his own musculature and found it without difficulty. He was a natural. He began to perspire in a healthy, deserving way. The sun rose quickly, liberating delicious scents of decomposition from the vegetation. In no more than an hour Malgas had raised three provisional heaps, each comprising four barrowloads, each at home on the exact spot the grid prescribed.

"Pssst."

Malgas's sense of communion with the fruits of his labour was so pronounced by now that for a moment he thought one of the heaps was addressing him in a cryptic language of gaseous vapours.

"Hey!"

There was no mistaking this human voice. He traced it to the small face of his wife, which jelled in a pie-slice of spokes and rim. He motioned the face to go away, but instead it grew larger and spoke again.

"Come here. I want to ask you something."

"Get back in the house."

He turned his attention to his work, but his rhythm had been broken: the rake twisted and fell on barren soil.

"What is it then? Be quick."

"Why aren't you at work?"

"I'm working."

"You know what I mean: who's minding the shop?"

"Van Vuuren."

"That monkey. What he knows about Hardware's dangerous. I can see him swilling our life's work down the drain."

Mr did not answer. He loosened one of his laces and tied it again in a double bow.

"Typical," she sniffed. "You'll give Him the shirt off your back, although you don't know Him from Adam, while your own family goes hungry."

"I have to help him."

"You're doing everything, you big baby. Look at Him. He's messing around, pretending to be busy."

Mr straightened his back wearily to watch his collaborator at work on the other side of the plot. Nieuwenhuizen lifted a bale of grass on his fork and shook a cloud of red dust out of it. Then he dumped the bale and thrashed around in the dust, snorting and waving the fork in front of him like a pair of horns. He had tied a bandanna with yellow polka dots over his mouth and donned a big-game hunter's hat with a leopard-skin band and the brim turned up sharply on one side. His dirty grey hair jutted out on that side like a scorched tuft of grass.

Nieuwenhuizen waved. Mr raised his hand to wave back, and realized just then that Nieuwenhuizen was simply fanning his face. So Mr's answering gesture had to be elided into a stretch instead and his sleeve had to mop up the sweat of his brow. This subterfuge only confused matters further, because it felt transparent and foolish. Nieuwenhuizen chuckled under his bandanna and speared another load of grass on his fork. With a flush of embarrassment darkening his tanned features, Mr went on raking. Mrs continued to speak to him, pointing out the folly of his ways, and the guile of His, but he ignored her and after a while she went away.

.   .   .

From her grandstand stool Mrs Malgas watched the day's proceedings with mixed emotions.

Her husband's part in the charade unfolding on the plot struck her as ridiculous and she very nearly laughed; yet as the day advanced and he toiled on with the same diligence, she felt obliged to take him seriously. It was as if a mantle of nobility had settled over him. She tried to brush this impression aside but it persisted, and she gazed upon him with new eyes, eyes which refused to distinguish between the man and what he was doing. She found herself becoming tearful.

There was something touching in the fact that the details of his person were familiar to her. His clothes contained him like a baggy second skin, imperfectly moulted: his overalls assumed the shape of his elbows and knees, and there were shiny bumps and ridges on his velskoene where the bones of his toes had pressed against the hide. Those were his favourite overalls, they had seen him through countless DIY projects, including the bricking up of the fireplace and the laying of the Slasto. She saw him kneeling, he looked over his shoulder and grinned. Each job had left a blemish on the cloth – a birthmark of enamel paint, a festering oil-stain, sutured cuts and tears, scabs of wood glue and Polyfilla. Just to look at them gave her pins and needles in her hands.

Now his steady exertions produced circles of sweat in his armpits, which spread out to meet a dark diamond in the small of his back, and the familiar khaki fabric changed slowly to chocolate-brown. This patient transformation flushed the hard-won scars to the surface; it also summoned up some elemental process of nature itself and brought more tears to her eyes, which she had to dab away resentfully with the hem of her skirt.

As the hours passed, Mr's neck seemed to redden visibly, but surely, she reasoned, that had more to do with the dust than the pale sunlight. More than once she was on the point of going to his rescue with a tube of Block Out and a pitcher of iced water, but she was held back by an intuition that this would implicate her in his foolhardy coalition with Him.

What made Nieuwenhuizen's trickery all the more despicable was that Mr was so glad to be of service, and therefore so easy to exploit. It was clear to Mrs that He was avoiding Mr. He always contrived to be in some neck of the woods where Mr was not. And whereas Mr did the work of two men, He did nothing but stir and shake, and scare up clouds of dust to obscure His own idleness. Now He was down in the gutter next to the road herding dry leaves into piles; now He was galloping on the spot and hurling His trident into the blue; now He was prancing up and down along the hedge, beating it with the flat of His spade, raking it with His hands and kicking it with His feet, so that its leaves flew up in clattering flocks and whirled in circles overhead. Where would they come to roost? Where they liked. What was the purpose of it all? To make more work for Mr.

"Lunch!" Mrs Malgas called feebly at one o'clock, and again, "Lunch!" But her summons fell on deaf ears.

In the mid-afternoon, when Mr had single-handedly raked the entire plot and was driving the stragglers from the moat around the tent, Nieuwenhuizen was stalking from heap to heap stirring up a new cloud of dust, which boiled over the hedge like a thunder-cloud, bruised and bloodied by the westering sun.

Nieuwenhuizen revolted Mrs Malgas. He was a source of dirt and chaos. She sealed all the windows, but His dust continued to sprout like a five o'clock shadow on the smooth surfaces of her home.

He's the salt of the earth, Nieuwenhuizen was thinking. A bit of a clod, but as solid as a rock for all that. And on top of it an eager beaver and a busy bee. He'll do. But as for that flimsy Mrs of his . . . lurking behind the wall as if she's invisible. She's no more than a scrap of tissue-paper. If you hold her up to the light you can see right through her.

An astute observer on higher ground may have understood the way in which Nieuwenhuizen kept his distance from Malgas in terms of the predictable revolution of the one man around the other, for when Malgas had raised his final heap Nieuwenhuizen was standing by to shake the excess dust out of it, and they straightened their backs and lowered their implements in unison. They walked in step – although Malgas was a single pace behind – to the middle of the plot, paused on the spot above the subterranean ruins of the anthill (VIE), and surveyed the landscape. It was an affecting sight – the stubbled earth with its ordered rows of mounds like so many graves. "How many?" Malgas wondered, while Nieuwenhuizen counted them under his breath.

A few meaningful glances were exchanged. Malgas went home to fetch his wheelbarrow. Mrs tried to attract his attention through the bedroom window, but he looked the other way. When he returned, whistling to disguise the unseemly *scree-scree-scree* of the axle, Nieuwenhuizen had rolled aside the hearthstones from the mouth of his tent to make space for the big heap.

In the gathering darkness they loaded the provisional heaps onto the barrow one by one and conveyed them to the depot. A jaundiced eye may have observed that Nieuwenhuizen did a great deal of pointing and waving, whereas Malgas wielded the fork and pushed the barrow. It was dark by the time they were done. The darkness brought with it, paradoxically, a boyish lightheartedness, which Nieuwenhuizen acknowledged by leaping onto the barrow and standing to attention, and Malgas confirmed by stepping once more into the breach and taking him on a tour of the site. When Nieuwenhuizen had had his fill of swaying hilariously and waving to unseen crowds of spectators, Malgas deposited him in the shadow of the heap.

The mountain of rotting vegetation towered over them. Here and there the turned leaves glowed like embers in the faded foliage, as if the whole mass would burst into flames if they so much as whispered near it.

With due caution, Nieuwenhuizen angled his face away and spoke for the first time since work had begun that morning. "Malgas, you've done a splendid job. I don't think I could have done it without you. I give you my word: nothing will grow here again, unless we want it to. Go home now. Rest. When you've refreshed yourself, come back, if you like, and we'll burn this heap to the ground, root and branch. Thanks a million, see you later."

Malgas understood intuitively the significance of this effusive utterance, just as he had appreciated the abbreviated chit-chat of the morning: it was in direct proportion to the satiated fullness of a job well done. So he himself embarked on a comprehensive response, which Nieuwenhuizen graciously allowed to run to three paragraphs before bidding him farewell and crawling without further ado into his tent.

Malgas went home.

Nieuwenhuizen lay on his back, with his head pillowed on one of his boots and his bare feet cushioned on his hat. A candle in a bully-beef tin rested on his stomach.

An insect was scaling the vault of mosquito-netting above him, and he followed its progress with interest. In everyday circumstances he would have squashed the intruder for reasons of hygiene, but he felt reckless tonight; and in any case, he had held the candle up a moment before and established that it was on the outside of the net. It was a perfectly ordinary bug, of the sort one might encounter in a cartoon wearing a waistcoat and spats. Its feet seemed disproportionately large and were shaped like exclamation marks.

The bug reached the apex of the tent, where the net was suspended from the tent-pole, and stopped. He willed it to keep going, over the top and down the other side, but it wouldn't budge. He flicked at it with his forefinger, hoping that it would curl itself into a ball and tumble down the way it had come, but it merely put out its feelers and clung to its position.

He held the flame close, to make out the expression on its face.

. . .

Meanwhile, Malgas stood on the scale in his bathroom, gazing down over the curvature of his belly at the figures on the dial, and tried to recall the wording of his recent thank-you speech.

He had started: "Ladies and gentlemen – I beg your pardon – Father. It gives me great pleasure to take this public opportunity of expressing my gratitude for . . ." But the rest of it was gone. He remembered some isolated words – "honour," "neighbourly," "vicinity," "collaboration," "endeavour." And he remembered what he was saying when Nieuwenhuizen interrupted him: "When the time comes—"

"Cheerio!"

Mrs Malgas came into the bathroom to talk some sense into her husband.

She found him wallowing in the muddy water, with his feet propped on the taps. He was preoccupied with his blisters, which had appeared in exactly the same spot on each hand: the web between thumb and forefinger. He prodded each blister in turn with the forefinger of the other hand, hoping that they would pop, but they held their shape tenaciously, like blobs of molten solder.

Mrs turned her attention to his feet. She didn't care much for them in this naked state, against a background of creamy ceramic tiles; she preferred them in shoes. They were childish feet, too soft and pink for the large brown body they were required to support. Their creased soles and shapeless toes made them look like underinflated bath toys.

His whole anatomy was stubbornly indifferent to her evaluations. She left him to soak.

But she was on hand, when he had dried himself, to rub some of her cold cream into the back of his neck, which was sunburnt after all.

The Buccaneer Steakhouse in the Helpmekaar Centre was one of the finest establishments of its kind anywhere. Its corporate motto was on everyone's lips: "Pleased to meet you, meat to please you." The Manageress, a Mrs Dworkin, and Mr Malgas were on first-name terms, so she was happy to take his order over the phone: two racks of ribs, one with chips and one with a baked potato.

"Nothing for me, thanks," Mrs said peevishly. "We always make do with a snack on Saturdays and I'm not going to change the habits of a lifetime just because of Him."

The Buccaneer was famous too for its cut-throat prices and speedy service, and within half an hour Malgas and Nieuwenhuizen were sitting on their stones at the foot of the dead mountain, in the moth-beaten light of the hurricane-lamp, with the distinctive customized polystyrene containers open on their knees. Nieuwenhuizen had chosen the baked potato and it steamed enticingly as he sliced it open with his plastic knife. He unwrapped a little brick of butter and dropped it into the gash.

"Baked in their jackets," Malgas said under his breath, repeating a phrase that Nieuwenhuizen had just used: "I've always loved them baked in their jackets." Malgas sighed and salted his chips. "It's better to give than to receive," he mused, "although receiving can also be good. Look, there's even vinegar in a little plastic bag – they think of everything." He bent his head over the ribs and breathed in a blend of BBQ Sauce and charbroiled lamb; by a happy coincidence, the Buccaneer's spicy marinade combined exquisitely with the delicate herby aroma of the heap . . . tarragon . . . cinnamon . . . kakiebos . . . It was perfect.

But what was that? Something medicinal had seeped into the mixture and threatened to spoil it entirely. Eucalyptus? No, lanolin? Camphor? Malgas sniffed again, and ascertained that the offensive smell was coming from the back of his neck! All at once he became acutely aware of how fresh and clean he was. There were creases in his shorts where creases had no business to be. There was a parting in his newly shampooed hair. The tops of his long socks were neatly folded – not once, but twice! "I've made an unforgivable booboo," he thought angrily, and forgave himself immediately. "The thought of bathing wouldn't have entered my head if she hadn't turned up her nose and run the water."

"Ingenious contraption," he said to cover his embarrassment.

"Notice the built-in hinges here, and the little triangular compartment in the corner for Sauce. Brilliant."

Nieuwenhuizen peered into the container, grunted, wiped his fingers on his safari suit and tore another rib from the rack.

When they had eaten their fill they moved their stones back in preparation for the bonfire.

"Say a few words, Father," Malgas suggested.

"Why not? I'm in a talkative mood." Nieuwenhuizen gathered his thoughts as he scoured the grease from his palms with a handful of sand, and then called for silence, cleared his throat, and began: "We have dined sumptuously, thanks to the generosity of our friend and colleague Malgas. Now let us enjoy a blazing fire and sit around it chatting amiably."

"Hear! Hear!" Malgas exclaimed. "Well spoken!"

Nieuwenhuizen took a match from a waterproof container, struck it, and dabbed the base of the heap with the flame.

It wouldn't burn.

"It so happens," said Malgas, reaching into the darkness and producing, with a flourish, a king-size pack of Blitz Firelighters.

Nieuwenhuizen shook his head resolutely.

It was a crestfallen Mr who barged through his house a few minutes later, snatched a key from a hook and went to the garage. Mrs followed him silently to the back door and waited there until he returned carrying a petrol tin.

"You be careful with that," she said.

Mr took two six-packs of beer from the fridge (Lions and Castles).

"You be careful with that too," she said, following in his footsteps to the front door and watching after him through the bars of the security gate. Then she went back to her stool in the darkened lounge.

Nieuwenhuizen took the petrol tin and departed for the top of the heap. Malgas wanted to go with him, but he wouldn't hear of it. "You'll get your boots dirty," he crowed. Malgas was left behind at the camp, staring dejectedly at his Hush Puppies. Nieuwenhuizen went up the heap in leaps and bounds and in no time at all he was standing on the summit. Instead of emptying the petrol into the "core," as Malgas had proposed, he raised the tin in an expansive toast and kicked his heels.

Malgas took the opportunity to break the Firelighters into sticks and spike the lower slopes. When that was done, he saw that Nieuwenhuizen was still occupied, so he slipped off his garters and pushed his socks down to his ankles. He ruffled his hair. He began to feel much better. Nieuwenhuizen stopped dancing and started pouring libations, first to the cardinal points of the compass and then to the lesser-known points in between. NNW, SSE, NWS. Malgas stretched himself out on the ground, rolled over a few times, and then looked up at the stars. They were far away, no argument. Mrs liked to describe them as pinpricks in a velvet tarpaulin. They had names, which the fundis were familiar with, and they were said to be "wheeling." Furthermore, your stars foretold. If you understood how to join them together, like puzzles, you could arrive at mythological beings and household names. "He probably knows just how to do it. He's travelled. Why don't I, when I know so much about the world? Over coffee I – blast! – the chocolate digestives!"

When Nieuwenhuizen eventually returned he was greeted by enthusiastic cries of "Speech! Speech!" but he waved the request aside. His adventures on the heap had had a marvellously soothing effect on him, for he patted Malgas between the shoulder-blades and handed him the matches. "Do the honours – you're the guest. I'll get the lights." He doused the hurricane-lamp.

Afterwards, when he recalled his conduct in these unusual circumstances, Malgas allowed himself a flush of pride. It would have turned out badly for him had he followed Nieuwenhuizen's lead and stooped to light the fire. In the heat of the moment, however, he was able to acquit himself with grace and composure. An image came into his mind – a match, like a tiny rocket, blazing an arc through space – and this godsend saved the day and impressed it on his memory as one of beauty and balance. His hand found exactly the gesture that was required to scrape the head of the match along the side of the box and propel it on its journey; the match, igniting as it entered the atmosphere and burning ever brighter as it flew, found precisely the triumphal trajectory that would bring it, when it was at its brightest, to the heap, which was by now embroiled in a miasma of volatile fumes; the heap sucked in its breath, soured with the smell of petrol, its tangled limbs shuddered, it gasped – and blurted out a tongue of flame so huge and incandescent that it turned night into day and extinguished the stars.

Nieuwenhuizen could not have been more astounded if Malgas himself had burst into flames. He pointed weakly at the stone next to him. Malgas lowered his bulk onto it and the two of them gaped in speechless wonder at the burning mountain.

At last the flames died down, the mountain began to collapse onto itself, squirting sparks into the insurgent darkness, and Nieuwenhuizen found his tongue.

"Pull your stone a bit closer and I'll tell you a story."

"Which reminds me," said Malgas. He reached casually into the shadows and brought forth the beers. They were still icy. Nieuwenhuizen punched Malgas's arm and chose a Castle, Malgas followed suit, and they popped them open.

"Cheers!"

They drank.

Malgas wiped the froth from his lips lavishly with the back of his hand. "Tell me about the old place," he prompted. "What made you tear up your roots and come all this way to start over? Do you have a dream? Tell me everything, don't leave out a single detail, I'm an empty vessel waiting to be filled. Also, I need facts, to win over the doubting Mrs."

These lines struck Malgas as among the finest he had ever uttered; there was no question that they were the most inspired he had addressed to Nieuwenhuizen so far. Nieuwenhuizen appreciated the speech too, and there was a touch of admiration in his expression as he tilted back his head, creating an oblique play of shadows across his features, stared into the fire, where a mass of twisted tongues were wagging, and murmured, "The Mrs."

"My wife."

"I remember." Pause. "Where to begin . . . Yes." He scuffed a burnt rib from the ashy edge of the fire with the toe of his boot. "Take this rib here, Malgas."

Malgas spat on his fingers and picked up the bone.

At that moment lights blazed in Malgas's lounge, a window burst open explosively, and Mrs Malgas was heard to shout, "Put out that fire at once! This is a smokeless zone! Give Him hell, Cooks!"

"She's gone too far this time," Malgas muttered, leapt to his feet and plunged into the darkness. As he fumed across the stubbled field, pressing his beer tin to his sunburnt neck, a broth of angry phrases seethed up in his throat, but the mere sight of his wife's trembling silhouette was enough to make him swallow it down. All he could manage as he hurried up to the wall was, "Put out that light! You're spoiling the fire."

"He's getting soot all over everything," she whined, and flustered like a paper cut-out against the window-pane. "The pool's turned black as ink. Look at your clothes! What have you been doing?"

"Haven't you done enough damage for one day?"

"This is a residential area." But the hurt note in his voice had disarmed her, and she rustled away and put out the light.

"He's coming out of his shell," Mr whispered urgently to the open window, "but one more insensitive intrusion could drive him back in again for good. Is that what you want? By the way – are there any biscuits in the house?"

There was no answer.

"Marshmallows?"

Silence. She had deserted her post.

For want of something better to do, he meandered back to the camp. In the distance the crooked figure of Nieuwenhuizen lay like a black branch beside a mound of flickering embers.

Mrs turned the TV set on and sat down in Mr's La-Z-Boy. The chair smelt of aftershave. It embraced her and made her feel small. The violet light from the screen, on which two men were swilling Richelieu brandy while they discussed money matters, lent the room the atmosphere of a butchery at night, glimpsed from a moving car. Pleased to meet you. She studied her thin forearms: her flesh looked bloodless and cold. "The pallor of death," was the phrase that came to mind, and it occurred to her to shout it out of the window.

"She sends her apologies, it won't happen again," said Malgas, seating himself on his stone and holding up the rib. "You were saying . . ."

"I was saying —"

"The pallor of death!"

"Then He danced around on the top, as if He was trying to trample the juice out of it, and He doused it with petrol, as if it was a tipsy-tart."

"For crying in a bucket, will you please stop telling me what he did! I was there, you know."

"Of course you were. I just thought you'd like a fresh perspective on events."

"I wouldn't. I'd like to forget the whole thing . . . I've never been so ashamed."

"You're still cross with me."

"We were getting on famously. He was opening up!"

Whether or not Mrs was to blame, Nieuwenhuizen lost his sense of purpose once again and went back to mooching on the plot.

His indolence did not bother Mr at all. "He's taking a well-earned break. He's in training for Phase Two: the actual building of the new house."

Mrs scoffed. "Break my eye. He's turned the environment into a wasteland, and now He's beating it senseless, pacing up and down in

His clodhoppers. You may think that nothing's happening, but I tell you, He's busy. Nothing will ever grow there again."

"Unless we want it to."

"What's that?"

"Nothing."

Even so, her allegations came back to him the next evening when he saw the huge heap of ashes left over from the bonfire and the flat earth signposted everywhere with crosses and arrows by Nieuwenhuizen's soles.

Every night Malgas joined Nieuwenhuizen at his modest new fireplace on the edge of the ash-heap; he no longer found it necessary to manufacture excuses for his visits, but he sometimes brought a small gift – a bracket or a hinge, a packet of screws or a brass lug, a plastic grommet or a fibreglass flange – as a token of his desire for constructive effort. Nieuwenhuizen stowed each one away with a smile.

Whenever Malgas inquired about the building operations, which was often, Nieuwenhuizen would chide him for his impatience. "All of this has been surveyed and subdued," he said, flinging out his arms to encompass his territory. "That in itself is no small thing. I'm not as young as I used to be. I need time to regain my strength."

"For Phase Two?"

"Of course."

It was after one of these routine exchanges that Nieuwenhuizen decided the time was ripe.

They were waiting for the pot to boil when Nieuwenhuizen went into action. He raked a red-hot nail as long as a pencil from the coals, elevated it with a pair of wire tongs, dunked it in his water drum, waved it to disperse the steam, inspected it meticulously, approved of it, and held it up by its sharp point. "Do you stock these?"

A tremor of foreboding ran through Malgas. He knew at once that a critical moment had been reached and he rose to the occasion like a fish to the bait. He narrowed his eyes professionally, took the nail, weighed it in one palm and then the other, tapped it on his thumbnail and held it up to his ear, sniffed its grooved shank and pressed its flat head to the tip of his tongue. "Unusual. I could requisition them for you . . . but surely you won't be needing such giants? If you were laying down railway lines or building an ark I could see the point of it, but for laths and joists and stuff like that something half this size would be twice as good."

"Don't give me a thousand words," Nieuwenhuizen said with a flicker of irritation. "I want three hundred of these, and so help me if they're not exactly like this one I'll send them back."

"I'll do it, relax. We have a saying at Mr Hardware: 'The Customer is always right.' But don't blame me—"

Just then the pot boiled, Nieuwenhuizen jumped up to wrest it from the coals, and Malgas swallowed the meat of his sentence, which was "—when your place doesn't have the professional finish, because the horns of these monsters are sticking out all over the show."

"The horns," said Mr to Mrs, "the *horns* of the *monsters*. That was what did it. He finally saw my point of view. If he builds that house of his one day he'll have me to thank."

particoloured. Castanets, chromium-plated, Clackerjack (regd. T.M.). Willow-pattern Frisbee. Mickey and Minnie, blessed by Pope (Pius). Pine-cone. Crucifix, commemorative, balsa-wood and papier-mâché, 255mm × 140mm. Calendar, Solly Kramer's, Troyeville, indigenous fauna painted with the mouth, 1991. Clock, Ginza, broken (TocH?)

It turned out that the factory couldn't deliver before the weekend because of a strike (living wage, benefits, maternity leave) and so Malgas made a detour through Industria on his way home from work and picked up the nails himself. Two hundred and eighty-eight of them came pre-packed snugly in two wooden boxes designed to hold a gross each, and the remaining dozen had been taped into a bundle and wrapped in brown paper.

Everything about this example of the packager's craft reassured Malgas. The grainy deal boards and ropy handles spoke of concern for safety in transit and overall effect; but there was attention to detail too, in the countersunk screw-heads and the spacing of the stencilled lettering: THIS SIDE UP. Rush-hour traffic gave him pause, and by the time he arrived at the site he was almost convinced that the gigantic nails would be perfect for the construction that lay ahead.

He loaded the boxes from the back of the bakkie into the barrow and wheeled them to the camp. Nieuwenhuizen had excused himself from this activity so that he could rummage through his portmanteau; Malgas therefore took the initiative and stored the boxes in a cool, dry place under the tree. Then he went back for the package containing the surplus dozen – the Twelve, as he thought of them. No sooner had he returned with those under his arm than Nieuwenhuizen found what he was looking for: a leather bandoleer, well loved but little used, to judge by the patina of dried Brasso on its buckle and the marrow of congealed dubbin and fluff clogging its many loops.

While Nieuwenhuizen strapped the bandoleer over his shoulder, Malgas took the initiative again and prised open the first box. He found a thick layer of shredded paper the colour of straw. Excellent. He threw the paper out and there they were: one hundred and forty-four of the finest nails money could buy, neatly stacked in rows of twelve, with the direction of the heads alternating stratum by stratum to compensate for the taper of the shanks. Even his exceptional sensitivity to packaging had not prepared him for this fastidious arrangement, and his admiration for the nails redoubled.

"Now that I see them here like this, in their proper context, I begin to see what you're driving at," Malgas mused. "There's something about them, I can't quite put my finger on it . . ."

Nieuwenhuizen looked into the box and smiled. He extracted one of the nails, blew a wisp of paper off it and slipped it into a leather loop. It fitted.

"Ah," said Malgas.

"Fill me up," Nieuwenhuizen commanded, spreading his feet and raising his arms as if Malgas was his tailor. He continued to smile benignly while Malgas loaded the bandoleer.

Malgas found it a satisfying task, punching out the dubbin marrow with the sharp point of each nail, wiping the goo off on his pants, and tugging the shank through until the head rested securely against the loop. Progressively, he was careful to research and develop an energy-conserving rhythm. There were thirty-six loops. Nieuwenhuizen bounced up and down on his toes, discovering his new equilibrium. Malgas was surprised his skinny legs didn't snap under the load.

"My hat."

Malgas unhooked the hat from a thorn, beat the dust out of it against his thigh, punched its crown into shape and placed it on Nieuwenhuizen's head. Nieuwenhuizen cocked it rakishly and asked, "How do I look?"

"Striking. What's the word . . . debonair."

"I like that. I feel debonair."

Nieuwenhuizen struck a few carefree poses and this gave Malgas a chance to examine his outfit more closely. He cut a fine figure. The only item that jarred was the bandoleer. In Malgas's opinion it was excessive. The longer he looked at it, the less he liked it. It was pretentious. A plain pouch on a leather belt would have served just as well. Now that he'd conjured up a pouch, he couldn't prevent a stream of plain images from gliding through his mind – the open face of a ball-peen hammer . . . a sturdy clod crumbling between a strong finger and thumb . . . a sap-stained scythe . . . a gush of chlorinated water from a hose . . . a sjambok . . . ploughshares . . . hessian pantaloons . . . hieroglyphs of mud dropping from the treads of a workmanlike boot. These uncalled-for images – who had summoned them? – and their stately passage – who was beating the drum? – gave him the creeps.

"You've got your nails," he said, rolling back the tide, "and rather too big than too small, I suppose. But, forgive me for pointing it out, you've got nothing to nail together. Forward planning is becoming more and more urgent. It's high time you ordered your materials: bricks, cement —"

"Enough is enough in any man's language!" Nieuwenhuizen said crossly. The fellow was already getting too big for his boots.

"Timber and allied products —"

"Shut up."

"Pardon?"

"Be still. I can't take this obsession with brass tacks a minute longer."

"Tacks?"

"You've got hardware on the brain, my friend, and it leaves you no room for speculation."

This outburst offended Malgas deeply. He had made a substantial contribution to recent developments, and Nieuwenhuizen knew it. Why was he distorting the facts? Nevertheless Malgas stammered an apology. "I'm just trying to be practical."

"You're so *practical*," said Nieuwenhuizen, who had not anticipated a defence, and repeated, "*You're* so practical," while he thought of what to say next. Then, without emphasis at all, "If you're as practical as you say you are, answer me this: Have you ever given a moment's thought to the shape and size of the new house?" By "ever" he meant since Malgas had been privy to his plans; and it must be said that this was exactly what Malgas understood him to mean. He went on regardless. "No you haven't, there's no need to state it. But let me tell you that I, for one, have to think about the new house all the time. Hardly a moment goes by that I don't think about it. I can see it before me as clear as daylight this very instant, even as I'm speaking to you. Can you see it? Hey? Can you name one little nook of it? Is it on a rack up here in the warehouse?" And he emphasized this final question rather crudely by rapping on Malgas's skull with his knuckles.

Such cruelty was out of character, and Malgas shrank from it in confusion and disappointment. "Not really . . ."

"There you are. That's what I'm talking about. No conception of the new house, but you're worrying yourself sick over what it's made of! You'd better sort out your priorities, man, or we won't be able to carry on collaborating on this project."

"I'm sorry Father," Malgas mumbled. "Collaborating," spoken in anger, had pierced him to the quick and the hurt was written all over his face. "I'm a simple soul, as you know. Now that you mention it, I'd love to see the new place. I'd give my eye-teeth to see it (as Mrs would say). But I'm not sure I can. You haven't given me clues. Shall I try anyway? Let's see . . . Is it a double-storey by any chance?"

"There-there, say no more." Just as suddenly as it had flared up, Nieuwenhuizen's rage died down again. "I'm the one who should apologize. I've expected too much of you, I thought you'd pick things up on your own, without guidance, and now we're both suffering because of my presumption. Perhaps it's not too late to make amends."

They sat on their stones with their knees almost touching. Both of them were suddenly apprehensive. Nieuwenhuizen opened and shut his mouth three and a half times, as if he wasn't sure where to begin, but at last took Malgas's hands in his own, kneaded them into one lump of clay, and said carefully, "Do you remember the old place I was telling you about on the night we met?"

Mere mention of that historic encounter, vividly evoked by the brambly clutches of Nieuwenhuizen's fingers, was enough to make Malgas throb with longing for days gone by, but he mastered his emotions and said matter-of-factly, "It was beyond repair. The plumbing was shot. If my memory serves me correctly, the boards under the bath were a shade of . . . green."

"Whatever. Point is: The new place will be nothing like that. In fact, it will be the absolute antithesis. Ironic. Where that place was old, for instance, this will be new. Where that was falling to pieces, this will be holding together very nicely thank you. That was rambling and draughty, this will be compact but comfortable. Spacious, mind, not poky, and double-storey . . ."

"I knew it!"

". . . to raise us up above the mire of the everyday, to give us perspective, to enable surveillance of creeping dangers. Make that triple-storey, don't want to cramp our style. Bathrooms *en suite*. Built-in bar. All tried and tested stuff, bricks and mortar and polished panels, the stuff of your dreams, none of this rotten canvas and scrap metal, transitional, all this, temporary, merely. Forward! Nothing tin-pot! Everything cast-iron! Bulletproof – we have to think of these things I'm afraid – with storage space for two years' rations. And on top of that wall-to-wall carpets in a serviceable colour, maybe khaki, and skylights and Slasto in the rumpus room. Materials galore, Malgas, right up your street. Malgas?"

Malgas opened his eyes, which were unnaturally bright.

"Can you see it?"

"I can't see *it* as such," said Malgas, reshaping two hands for himself, one with the other, and packing them around the brambles, "but I can see that it will be a fantastic place! I've made a start. Thank you."

"That's much better. Now what do I owe you for the nails?"

"Forget it."

"I insist."

"I really couldn't."

particoloured. Boot, camouflage, combat. Chopper, Soviet-made, collapsible. Traditional weapon: assegai, knopkierie, panga, pike, pole,

stick, stone, brick, mortar-board, fountain-pen, paper-clip, rubber
stamp, gavel, sickle, spade, rake, hoe, spoke, knitting-needle, crochet-
hook, darning-egg, butter-knife, runcible spoon, pot, pan, gravy-boat,
whisk

Nieuwenhuizen's hat hung at an impudent angle in the thorn-tree and
his boots stood side by side on the ground below with their tongues
sticking out. Taken together hat and boots suggested nothing so much
as an invisible man.

Nieuwenhuizen in person, the object of the invisible one's scru-
tiny, stood at attention nearby – in the north-western corner of block
IF – gazing candidly into the sunrise. Until this moment the sun had
been rising irrecoverably like a child's balloon, but now it stood still,
surprisingly enough, as if a dangling string had caught in the branches
of the hedge.

Although he appeared to be considering the implications of this
earth-shattering improbability, Nieuwenhuizen's thoughts were
in fact on the top of his head and the soles of his feet, which were
developing pins and needles. He furrowed his forehead and shimmied his eyebrows in an effort to flush some blood into his scalp. He
stretched his toes. He flexed his left hand, which was in his pocket: that
at least was in good condition and ready for the task that lay ahead.
His right hand, by contrast, was frozen into a claw around his flint
hammer, and felt numb and unwieldy. To crown it all, the bandoleer,
with its freight of nails, began to hurt his shoulder.

He was on the point of conceding defeat and retreating to his tent, when the sun escaped from the grasp of the hedge and bobbed up into the sky.

"Optical illusion," he said with a sigh of relief, and sallied forth.

He stepped off with his right foot and took six stiff paces. The earth felt unusually firm and steady. When his left foot came down for the third time, in the middle of IE, he flung the hammer in his right hand forward with all his might, pivoted on his heel, toppled sideways, flew into the air, flapped after the hammer like a broken wing, went rigid as a statue in mid-air, hung motionless for a long, oblique instant, and crashed to earth with a cry of triumph. He levered himself up and located the impression of his heel on the ground; then the starch went out of him and he flopped down on all fours to get a good look at the mark. It was shaped like a comma, with a bloated head and a short, limp tail. He took a nail from the bandoleer and pressed its point into the comma. Then, swinging his right arm like a piece of broken furniture, he hammered the nail into the ground.

Sparks flew! He was satisfied.

He closed his eyes, stretched out both arms and turned in circles, clockwise, counting under his breath, "Two thousand and one, two thousand and two, two thousand and three . . ." At this point he stopped, ran on the spot, fell on his knees, patted the earth with his palms, pummelled it with his fists, sniggered, jumped up again and began to turn in circles, anti-clockwise, "Two thousand and three, two thousand and two, two thousand and one . . . There, that's better."

He fixed his eyes on the stunted appendage that passed for the chimney of Malgas's house, extended his arms once again like a tightrope artist, and proceeded in measured paces across the plot. The hammer in his right hand disturbed his balance and introduced an unsightly wobble into his limbs; but his head for a change was completely still. He gritted his teeth and kept going, step after step, until at last his whole frame was vibrating like a dowsing-rod. With a final effort of will he threw himself into the air, cracked his heels together and struck the earth with his head. Light-bulbs flickered in his brain. He saw the firmament, tricked out with stars in pastel colours, and three scrawny birds, scavengers, flapping tiredly in a circle. Then everything went dark.

When he came to his senses his head was throbbing. He had no idea how much time had been lost, although he could have worked it out easily enough from the position of the sun. Sitting up and looking about, he was cheered to discover on the ground a perfectly legible imprint of the back of his head. Auspiciously, it was in VID. He pulled a hot, oily nail from a loop and bashed it into the ground in the middle of the depression.

The planting of this second nail left him drained and disorientated, so he paced the next three out sedately, marking the spot for each one with his elbow as if he was testing the baby's bath-water and tapping them in as if they were made of glass. It happened that the fifth nail lay in a far-flung corner, IA, where the hedge met the Malgases' wall, and the desolate surroundings weighed so heavily upon him that he resolved to find a resting-place for nail number six in the more hospitable neighbourhood of his own homestead.

Accordingly, he put his left foot in front of his right, bent his knees, and swept his arms up behind his back like a diver. He raised the toes of his left foot and the heel of his right. Then he swung his arms forward and brought his hands together in front of him, clutching his flint, at the same time raising the heel of his left foot and the toes of his right. Then he went back to the first position, breathed in, held it to a count of ten, returned to the second position and breathed out. Then he rocked from the second position to the first and back again five times, and once more for luck. And then he ran forward, hopped, skipped, dodged, ducked, rolled head over heels, swerved, leap-frogged over the ash-heap and bore down upon the thorn-tree as if he intended to pass straight through it.

At the last moment he bounced on the balls of his feet – he was warm as toast by now, he was doggerel in motion – and leapt onto an overhanging branch. It was a pin-point landing, and he sustained just one superficial scratch on his shin. He quickly located the launching site and, hanging upside-down from his heels, was able to position the sixth nail (IIA) before dropping down to dispatch it with a few assertive blows. Fireworks!

When it came to lucky number seven, he was bold enough to attempt a backflip with a half-twist over the tent, nearly pulled it off, belly-flopped, and consoled himself with a catnap.

"Mr!"

Mrs Malgas, whose turn it was to make the morning coffee, was filling the kettle at the sink when Nieuwenhuizen came to her attention. The sight of him on an empty stomach all but robbed her of the power of speech.

Mr shuffled through in his towelling dressing-gown. "Where's the fire?"

All she could say was: "Him!"

Mr looked out of the window. He saw Nieuwenhuizen going round in circles. This was something entirely new. What in heaven's name was he up to now?

Mr sat Mrs down at the table and poured the coffee. Once she was clutching her favourite mug Mrs managed to get a grip on herself as well, and within a minute had recovered well enough to give a full account of the incident.

"It's unspeakable," she said, "but I'll do my best. I was standing where you are now, yes there, and I happened to look out of the window, which is only to be expected, one can hardly help it, and what do you think I saw?"

"Him?"

"That's right. At first He was just standing there with His back to me, in His usual impolite way. But without warning He flung Himself down face first, and started to heave and thump this way and that in the throes of an ungovernable lust, as if He meant to penetrate the very earth upon which we stand."

"He was doing some P.T. He's building himself up for Phase Two."

"He was thrusting and thumping nineteen to the dozen! You can still see the dust."

"Probably push-ups."

"Afterwards, He hurled Himself to His feet again, and strutted up and down as immodestly as ever."

Nieuwenhuizen was still waddling in circles, with his chest puffed up and his feet turned out.

"I don't see anything untoward," said Mr.

"It's too late now. If you'd come when I called you, you'd have seen it with your own eyes, and you wouldn't be so quick to defend Him."

"There's more to this than meets the eye. I know for a fact that he's afraid of sinking through the crust of the earth. Yet you say he forced himself upon it. It's a contradiction."

"Don't patronize me."

Nieuwenhuizen lay down on his back with his arms flung wide and his feet crossed. He stared into the streaming eye of the sun. Then he flopped over on his stomach, spread-eagled his arms and legs, and put his ear to the ground.

"I'm sure there's a perfectly simple explanation," said Mr.

"My word counts for nothing in this house." Mrs flounced to the lounge to finish her coffee.

Nieuwenhuizen raised his head and squinted at the topsoil under his nose. His ear pressing against the sand had created a small relief map, a flat-topped mountain surrounded by whorled hillocks and vales. He peeped through his eyelashes. Some pebbles assumed the appearance of boulders piled at the foot of the mountain; then his nostrils stirred up a dust-storm; and that blew over, leaving in its wake a dry blade of grass that looked just like a wind-wracked palm-frond.

He stuffed a hand into a crack in his side and pulled a nail from the bandoleer. He pressed it into the mountain, just deep enough so that it would stand upright on its own. In this prone position driving the nail in was no easy task. He flailed his arms like a drowning victim.

"Tsk! I might have known!" Mr exclaimed. "He's making a plan!"

He stomped through to the lounge. "I've cleared up the mystery, Mrs: he's making a plan. For the new house. Remember?"

"Bully for Him." Her coffee was cold, but she took a sip anyway so that she could exchange a knowing look with the mug-frog.

"Did I mention the nails?"

"Monsters."

"All along I've been thinking he wants them for the actual construction – and here he is, making a plan with them. It goes to show that you can't take anything for granted with him. He's so crafty."

"He's a show-off." She went to her room.

Nieuwenhulzen walked backwards and sat down.

"I think I'll pitch in," said Mr. He pursued Mrs to the bedroom. She was lying on the bed with the candlewick bedspread pulled up to her chin. He said to her: "I think I'll pitch in."

"What on earth for?"

"He needs me."

"He's doing just fine on His own. He told you He didn't need your help. He spurned you."

"Don't be petty. You've seen for yourself what a struggle it is for him. Another pair of hands will make all the difference, but he finds it hard to ask, because he prides himself on his independence."

"I can see the two of you, lying there thumping like a couple of gaffed barbels."

Malgas donned his overalls and went next door. He found Nieuwenhuizen lying on his side in the shade under the hedge. He appeared to be sleeping, but as Malgas drew near he raised his head and opened his eyes.

"Father."

"Malgas."

"Making a plan, I see."

"Trying."

"Ingenious, if you don't mind me saying so."

"Not at all. Thanks."

"Plans are interesting. Fascinating, actually. I suppose I'll always have a soft spot for materials, it's in my blood, along with packaging, but as I get older I find I become more and more curious about the planning side of things."

"Stop beating about the bush," Nieuwenhuizen said, sitting up and dusting off his sleeve. "What do you want?"

"To give you a hand here, if you'll have me."

Nieuwenhuizen looked dubious. "I don't know. Are you ready for it, I wonder? I don't want to rush you."

"I'm as ready as I'll ever be. I can't see the new house yet, but it goes without saying that *you* can. And I'm eager to learn. I have a great hunger and thirst for knowledge of the house. If necessary I'm prepared to start at the bottom and work my way up. You'll teach me everything you know, and in the mean time I'll fetch and carry the tools and so on. I took the liberty of bringing this mallet – with rubber you don't damage the heads."

"I'm not sure . . ."

"Look at it this way: I have my own field of expertise, or 'know-how' as we call it in the trade, and one day I'll be able to repay every little kindness shown me in these difficult times. Just shout: Mr Hardware, A World of Materials under One Roof."

Nieuwenhuizen sprang to his feet. He stuck one of his skinny fingers through a loop of the bandoleer and said, "You're just in time to reload me. I didn't want to ask, but since you're offering . . ."

They walked towards the camp, where the boxes of nails were standing one on top of the other, and Malgas ventured to walk at Nieuwenhuizen's side.

With Malgas's enthusiastic assistance, the mapping out of the ground-plan proceeded apace. A less elaborate drafting procedure was called for now, and the acrobatics of the early morning therefore gave way to more conventional pacing and pointing; and while before there had been as many different marks as there are parts of the human body, now there was one standardized sign, a plump full stop made with the heel, so that the apprentice could not fail to recognize it.

Malgas politely commandeered the bandoleer and took charge of placing the nails according to Nieuwenhuizen's wishes. Although he assumed that the grid system was finally coming into its own, he accepted the given division of labour and made no attempt to decipher the plan: he concentrated instead on inserting the nails expertly. Now was the time to explore the ins and outs of the undervalued art of hammering. As he perfected his swing, he brought the effort required for each insertion down to a single preliminary tap to make the nail stand on end; two decisive double-fisted smashes to sink it; and a concluding salvo of tiny blows to ensure that the head was protruding above the surface to the specified extent (the thickness of his thumb).

Nieuwenhuizen sang a song. It was his tent-pitching song, and its haunting tones brought the bitter-sweet memory of his advent into Malgas's mind as clearly as if it was yesterday. However, it also broke his concentration, and he was relieved when Nieuwenhuizen fell silent and focused on the measurements.

As for Nieuwenhuizen, when he judged that Malgas had mastered the full stop, he added the colon and the ellipsis to his repertoire, although he was careful to keep the combinations simple. Malgas took it in his stride.

The world turned. The sun trundled like a brass ball across the leaden bowl of the sky. They didn't miss a beat.

At one o'clock Mrs Malgas flung her window open and offered "Lunch!," and was turned down by the muted rhythm of the mallet and the sky resounding like a cracked gong. She shut the window and went away.

Hour after hour, Nieuwenhuizen fumed over the plot, disseminating his indelible punctuation. Malgas dogged his footsteps, discharged volley after volley of nails, reloaded the bandoleer again and again, and never once complained.

Night fell at last. The second box of ammunition was broached. By now the nails had been scattered far and wide; their heads glistened everywhere, like tiny pools holding the lees of the light. Still there was work to be done.

Nieuwenhuizen lit the lamp and carried it with him, swinging wildly from one hand, as he paced. He held it so close to the action that he singed the hairs on Malgas's arm. And through it all he kept demanding, "More light!" and imploring the moon to rise, which it didn't. Then Malgas took the unprecedented step of running a lead-light through his kitchen window (Mrs wept) and they soldiered on with new vigour. In the light cast by the cowled globe Nieuwenhuizen acquired the stature of a giant, striding across immense, uninhabited plains, while Malgas, shambling after him, brought his master's mallet crashing down on nails as tall as flagstaffs.

Finally the moment came when Malgas reached into the box and grasped nothing but a mulch of shredded paper. Permission was granted for him to tear open the brown-paper bundle containing the Twelve. He intended to slip these too into the bandoleer, but Nieuwenhuizen intervened. The final dozen required special attention.

Nieuwenhuizen curled the forefinger and thumb of his left hand into a loophole and peered through it with his right eye. He panned across the entire landscape, apprehending each and every nail both as a distinct entity and as part of a complex pattern, computing the most abstruse distances and obtuse angles, and considering entirely unexpected relationships between them. Then he took the lead-light and explored the spangled darkness, pointing out nooks and crannies among the glittering constellations underfoot, and Malgas flew the nails to those spots.

It was done.

A half-jack of Johnny Walker and a nip of Drambuie had been laid down in the portmanteau and now came to light. "I've been saving them for a rainy day," Nieuwenhuizen explained, "but this star-crossed evening will do." He also produced a cocktail shaker, made out of a lampshade and a surgical glove, and in two shakes they had their feet up and were sipping cocktails out of tin mugs.

"It's a little late for sundowners, and a little early for nightcaps, but cheers anyway. To you and yours!"

His host's gratitude, so deeply felt and tastefully expressed, brought a lump to Malgas's throat, and he had to wash it down with a slug of the mixture before he could voice his own appreciation for everything.

Then Nieuwenhuizen said, "If you don't mind I'd like to go over the plan now, while it's fresh. If you're not ready for such heady stuff, perhaps you should block your ears. Better still, go home to the Mrs. I don't want to cause any trouble. Go on, take your drink with you."

"I'd be grateful if I could stay," Malgas protested. "Plans aren't my thing, I admit, I'm a supplier at heart – but I've got to start somewhere."

"That's my boy, I was hoping you'd say that. Are you comfortable? Okay . . . where to begin? Yes: the corners. See that nail there, on the edge of the shadows, and the two behind it, with their heads together?

Well, that, my Malgas, delimits the north-eastern extremity of the rumpus room."

Malgas gasped.

"That one there, in line with the letter-box, is the left-hand what's-its-name . . . jamb of the front door. Not that one, *my* left."

The long shadow of Nieuwenhuizen's forefinger brushed over the smooth heads of the nails, weaving a web of diaphanous intent in which Malgas was willingly ensnared and cocooned. Nieuwenhuizen's hand, moving now with the delicate poise of a spirit-level, now with the brute force of a bulldozer blade, levelled terraces and threw up embankments, laid paving and plastered walls. With a touch, his skittery fingers could open a tracery of light and air in a concrete slab, and through it his papery palms would waft a sea breeze laden with salt and the fruity scents of the orchard. Apricot, blueberry, coconut-milk. He made it seem so simple.

He began with the situation and dimensions of the rooms, which were many and various. Then he took the rooms one at a time and elaborated on the location of doors and windows, built-in cupboards, electricity outlets, switches and light fixtures. He catalogued special features, such as burglarproofing, air-conditioning and knotty-pine ceilings. He dwelt upon the observation deck, the rumpus room and the bomb shelter, all of which, he assured Malgas, had an integral place in the conception.

"Fascinating," said Malgas, shaking off the narcotic effects of the presentation. "But I must admit that I still can't really see it. There's no point in lying about it, is there?"

"Of course not. You're finding it heavy going because the plan isn't quite finished; we've still got to join up the dots. When that's done it will all become clear. For the time being, don't lose heart, and practise, practise, practise. You know what they say."

"I'll try. But I feel so clumsy."

"Let me give you a tip. I find that it helps if I . . . I shouldn't be telling you this, I'm rushing you again. Let's wait until you begin to see on your own."

"No, no, please go on," Malgas pleaded, "I'll stop you if it's too much too soon."

"Just say when. I find that it helps if I think along the following lines: layers, levels; colour schemes, cutaway views and cross-sections; also surfaces and sheens; and last but not least, varnishes and veneers. Consider: the letter-box of the new house. No minor detail, this. The letter-box. Not exactly a replica of the new house itself, not exactly a scale model, that's too obvious, but . . . reminiscent. An Alpine chalet, of the kind you associate with the better sort of pleasure resort, but not thatched. A roof of painted metal, red, but faded to a cooldrink colour, strawberry – no, that's not it – faded to a – yes, this is good – to a pale shade of mercurochrome, a grazed knee after two or three baths, and just beginning to blister. The rusty door, for example, yes, I like this too, the rusty door has the scabrous texture of a cold sore. No, no: impetigo. Are you with me? You open the door, *scree*, you look in, the walls are galvanized, hygienic, hard-wearing and maintenance-free. There's a letter in the box, a tilted plane of pure white, you reach in, your hand glides over the floorboards, tongued and grooved meranti, sealed against the elements, yes —"

"When."

Malgas paused at the letter-box. He looked in through a sash-window. Empty.

As he made his way home he heard Mrs saying, Where is everybody? Does He have relatives? He never gets visitors. What does He want with that letter-box? Is He on mailing lists? Does He get items marked Private and Confidential? Manila envelopes and cardboard tubes, magazines in plastic wrappers, tax returns, advertising flyers, free literature with a money-back guarantee?

Mr came in from the wilds reeking of whisky and gunpowder. His palms were covered in blisters and he showed them off like handfuls of medals.

"What have you done to your thumbs?" Mrs demanded.

But he silenced her with a speech about the plan, the mystery of the new house, and the special techniques Nieuwenhuizen had revealed to him for understanding it. Very impressive it was, she had to agree. Gratified, he marched to the bathroom, flung off his overalls and admired his aches and pains in the mirror. Then he sat in the tub with his knees jutting out of the foam like desert islands, while Mrs soaped the broad beach of his back.

"I think I understand about the plan," she said, "and the palace fit for an emperor, even though I don't approve. But what's this about special techniques?"

"I probably shouldn't be telling you at all, but I'll go over it once more." He dipped the sponge in the water and held it up. "Take this sponge, Mrs. Solid, not so? Look at the surface here, that's it, the surface. Full of holes, craters yes? Craters yes, mouths, leading to subsurface tunnels, souterrains, catacombs, sewers – yes, I like that – twists and turns. Squeeze it out, go on, *schquee,* full of water, not any old water, second-hand bathwater, I should think so, yes."

"I've never heard such nonsense in my life! Really. I wish you could hear yourself."

"You'd appreciate it if you'd been in the wars like me." He let in more hot to cauterize his wounds.

While Mr was shovelling down his cold supper Mrs said, "You used to have your feet on the ground. That's why I married you. That's why you went into Hardware."

This set Mr thinking about Nieuwenhuizen again, and he replied, "I think he's a bit of a hardware man himself, you know, although he won't admit it. He's good with his hands. And this stuff about varnish and veneer, it boils down to materials. Doesn't it?"

One hand poured fuel on the other. Then the pouring hand flicked an orange lighter and the doused hand burst into flames. The burning hand! Then the flicking hand snuffed out the flames with a silver cloth. The charred hand! Then the snuffing hand peeled off a charred glove.

The pink flesh of the inner hand. The perfect hand! The perfect hand turned this way and that, and waved (hello or goodbye), a V sign (for victory, approval, or vulgar derision), thumbs up (sl. excl. of satisfaction), finger language (up yours!), fist language (Viva!), so that you could see it was perfect.

Mr fell asleep in his La-Z-Boy with the TV glaring. Mrs went to the bedroom, seated herself before the winged mirror of her dressing-table and said, "Although I appear to be thin and small, and fading away before your eyes, I am a substantial person. At least, it feels that way to me."

Her pale reflection repeated the lines in triplicate.

Yet she saw through the pretence. It was clear: she was made of glass. And under the bell-jar of her skin, in a rarefied atmosphere, lashed by electrical storms and soused by chemical precipitations, her vital organs were squirming.

In the middle of that same night, somewhere around three, as if he hadn't endured enough already, it happened that Malgas was boiled alive in a gigantic cauldron. Nieuwenhuizen was in there too, fully clothed. It was rough. Logs of carrot and cubic metres of diced potato swirled up on torrents of bubbles and buffeted them. Hot spices seared the skin off their faces and onion-rings strangled them. They clung together in the seething liquid. A pea the size of a cannon-ball caromed off the side of the pot and struck Malgas in the eye. He went under once. Twice. The third time he grabbed hold of Nieuwenhuizen and dragged him down for luck. Now it was every man for himself. Nieuwenhuizen seized a bouquet garni bound in muslin and held it over Malgas's face. Bubbles, Bisto, Malgas began to lose consciousness. His lungs filled up with gravy, gasp, gasp, sinking, spinach, must hold on, everything went brown . . . He awoke in a sweat, clutching his pillow.

The stock left a bitter taste in his mouth, and he had to go to the bathroom to rinse it out. On the way there he made a detour past the lounge window to confirm that Nieuwenhuizen had never existed at all. But no sooner had he parted the curtains than a match flared and the hurricane-lamp bloomed into light.

Holding the lamp high, rocking it portentously like a censer, Nieuwenhuizen circled the ash-heap. After three circuits, he waded into the ashes and scuffed a clearing with his boots. He took a nail folded in a bandanna from his pocket, unwrapped it under the light, kissed it, knelt and pressed its point into the ground. It kept falling over, and in the end he had to prop it up with a forked twig. For a while he was silent, on his knees in the grey surf. Then he began to sway backwards and forwards from the waist, solemnly, gathering momentum slowly, extending his range, until at length his bony forehead, at the limit of its forward swing, began to meet the head of the nail. And by these means he kowtowed it into the ground. When the ashes had settled he killed the lamp and went back to bed.

Mr recognized the secret nail at once: it was the one Nieuwenhuizen had annealed in the fire on the night he placed his order. It was the odd nail out, and yet it was the very model of a nail. Fire and ash. What did it signify? He made a note of its secret location (IIIC) but still he was baffled. Then all at once bafflement gave way to an embarrass-ing abundance, and his empty mind was cluttered with possibilities: chains of mnemonics shaped like knuckle-bones and skeleton keys; a tissue of lies, knitted on nails and pencils; the family tree of fire, leaves of flame, seeds of ash. He pushed these shop-soiled articles aside and found a small, hard certainty, which he strung on the scale of intimacy between Nieuwenhuizen and himself: communion.

The plan was incomplete and it lay fallow. Nieuwenhuizen said it was maturing.

Mr Malgas spent all his spare time practising to see the new house, racking his brains to recall Nieuwenhuizen's guidelines and finding them all reduced to the unhelpful ambiguity of dreams.

One night, after Nieuwenhuizen had sent him home and retired, Mr Malgas had such a powerful need to pursue his observations that he took a torch and crept back onto the plot in his gown and slippers.

Shielding the beam with a cupped palm, he examined the clearing in the ashes, and there he thought he saw the head of the secret nail glimmering. In the presence of this mystery, the key to the new house and its creator – he could reach out and touch it if he chose – his courage failed him and he almost fled. Steady, Malgas. He wiped the beam of the torch slowly across the plan, and here and there, here and there the nails glinted, as if the land had been sown with petty cash.

He became bolder. He drew the beam from nail to nail, emulating Nieuwenhuizen's self-assured gestures, hoping to trace the outlines of just one room, a passage way, an alcove that would presage a dwelling. The nails winked and told him nothing. He could not make out even a fragment of the blueprint nailed to the ground.

Growing increasingly agitated, and casting the need for stealth to the wind, he began to stride back and forth, doodling the finger of light from one shiny marker to the next, foraging in the outlying areas for any he might have missed and stirring them into significance. And even though there was no sign of the new house, he found himself whispering vehemently, "Bedroom . . . yes! Double bed, king-size . . . yes! Bathroom *en suite*, shower cubicle . . . yes! yes!" When this approach failed to produce tangible results, it came to him that everything would be crystal clear if only he could view it from above, from some vantage-point like the anthill – no, that had ceased to exist – like the tree – no, no, that was full of thorns – like the roof of his own house! The impropriety of this idea, especially at such a late hour, brought him down to earth with a bump, and he quickly went home.

Nieuwenhuizen saw him go, from the mouth of the tent, and laughed like a drain; Mrs Malgas saw him coming, from the lounge window, with tears in her eyes, and hurried back to bed, where she pretended to be sleeping.

"Queen-size . . . never! Over my dead body!"

Mr Malgas tossed and turned, trying to remember the disposition of the nails and chart them dot for dot, but try as he might, his markers were swept away repeatedly by avalanches of punctuation.

Never fear, Malgas practised harder than ever.

And late one afternoon his persistence paid off. He had been criss-crossing the plan for an hour on end with his chin on his chest and his hands behind his back. Nieuwenhuizen was sitting at the fireplace, in which some split logs and balls of newspaper had been stacked in a pyre, peeling a clutch of lumpy roots for a stew. He had a tolerant smile on his face. Suddenly a light bulb blazed in a dusty recess in Malgas's mind, and he understood why he could not see the new house: it was underground!

"What a clot I've been, assuming that these nails mark the foundations, when it's perfectly obvious – once you cotton on to it – that they mark the chimney-pots, gutters, eaves, spires, domes and dormers, to name but a handful of your more prominent roof-top features. This nail here is clearly a television aerial. Two pigeons over there – that's a nice touch – a family of gargoyles, and here's a weather-cock."

Malgas felt the Cape Dutch gables of the subterranean house thrusting up against his soles. He took off his shoes. That did the trick. In a transport of heightened sensitivity, he tottered along a gutter, clambered up a steep, shingled roof and established himself next to a chimney with a cloud of smoke swirling about his knees.

Then he came to his senses and found that he was standing in the ash-heap.

Nieuwenhuizen, who was crouching nearby dicing his roots on a chopping-block with a hand-beaten copper cleaver, called out, "Good one, Mal! You're getting the hang of it."

Malgas was embarrassed.

He went home looking for sympathy, but Mrs glared at his laddered socks, rattled her newspaper and gave him a lecture: "Terrible times we're living in. Death on every corner. The forces of destruction unleashed upon an unsuspecting public. Trains colliding, ferries capsizing, mini-buses overturning, air liners plummeting from the sky on top of suburbs, massacres in second-class railway coaches, public transport in general becoming unsafe, rivers bursting their banks, earthquakes shaking everything up, volcanoes erupting, bombs exploding, businesses going bang, buildings collapsing, among other things. And on top of all this, as if we don't have enough on our plates, a lunatic on our doorstep. And on top of the top, his accomplice under our own roof."

"It could be worse."

"It could be better. Look here: BOF! in a bubble. Sometimes I don't know whether to laugh or cry. Here, a cat cracking jokes in English. Ducks in suits and ties, a dog in a flashy sports coat, a mouse driving a car. And here's your foolish friend to a T: this man is walking on thin air, if you don't mind, until someone points it out to him . . . and *that* makes him fall like an angel."

. . .

Out of the blue shadows of a Sunday afternoon, Nieuwenhuizen let it be known that the plan had reached maturity. Malgas's joy in this news was premature and short-lived. Apparently, the fact that the plan was mature did not imply that the actual construction was about to begin; rather, it meant that the plan could now be *completed*, and unfortunately Nieuwenhuizen alone was qualified to perform this delicate operation. He sent Malgas packing, with strict instructions to lie low until his presence was requested at the official unveiling.

"I've got your interests at heart," Nieuwenhuizen said. "You've been a sport, but there's really no point in seeing bits and pieces of the plan. To get the proper effect you need to see the whole thing, fully assembled."

Feeling that he had unwittingly passed some test, and failed another, Malgas said, "Thank you, thank you," and left.

Nevertheless, as soon as he arrived home he ordered a beer shandy and a bowl of salted peanuts from Mrs and when she went to do his bidding usurped her stool behind the net curtain.

She did not protest. "I'm tired of humouring Him anyway. He loves being the centre of attraction, like someone else I know."

Mr Malgas had hardly installed himself when Nieuwenhuizen popped out from behind the thorn-tree with a ball of string in his hand. After a brief search he squatted down and attached the end of the string to the head of a nail, tying several knots of different kinds – Mr Malgas spotted a clove-hitch and two grannies – and tugging hard to make sure they held. Mr Malgas judged correctly that this was no ordinary nail and made a note of its position (IE), but he had no way of knowing that it was the inaugural nail, the very first one to take its place in the plan.

Nieuwenhuizen stuck his index fingers into either end of the cardboard tube on which the string was wound and swung out his forearms like hinged brackets. He raised them and lowered them a few times, as if he was testing out a patent string-dispenser. Apparently the gadget worked, for he now walked confidently backwards, playing out the string as he went, until he bumped into Malgas's wall. He chose another nail and looped the string around it, performed a difficult manoeuvre with the whole ball which unexpectedly resulted in a slip-knot, and pulled that tight.

Mr Malgas's standpoint may have been comfortable, but it was also limiting, and he found that he couldn't determine what block of the grid this second nail was in. Oh well, it didn't seem to matter. The line between Point A and Point B (Obscured), as he spontaneously renamed them, was so beautiful, so true, that he laid his eyes on it with love. Upon such a line one wished, without even thinking about it, to erect a noble edifice. This desire stretched the line so tight that it hummed with possibility and he grew afraid that it would snap.

Nieuwenhuizen, meanwhile, had trotted off to the hedge in search of another nail. He dropped down on all fours and scrambled in among the woody stems, thrashed around in an uproar of splintering twigs and dust, re-emerged boots first, picked himself up, shook himself like a spaniel, and set off again, wagging the line behind him.

The technique was clumsy, Mr Malgas thought, as his initial infatuation with it wore off, but the intention was clear: this new line, B

(Obscrd) to C, proposed a wall. It was a little too close to his own wall for comfort, perhaps, but what the hell, it was also a beautiful line.

Again and again, Nieuwenhuizen stooped, looped and knotted, and Mr Malgas, catching glimpses of grand columns and entablatures between the lines, muttered, "Yes! Yes!" and struck his palm with his fist.

But then, without warning, Nieuwenhuizen sundered the beautiful line between A and B (Obs) as if it had no more substance than a shadow. The components of the new house that Mr Malgas had been building up, all labelled clearly with letters of the alphabet, disengaged their joints with doleful popping noises (*oompah*) and drifted deliberately apart.

"Use your imagination, Malgas!" he rebuked himself. "Don't be so bloody literal."

Nieuwenhuizen went from nail to nail, stooping and looping. From time to time, when he stood back to observe the emerging plan, Mr Malgas studied it too, climbing up on his stool and peeping from under the pelmet in the hope that added elevation would bring greater insight. Nothing worthy of being called a new house suggested itself, neither rising above the ground nor sinking below. Something resembling a room would appear, a string-bound rectangle of the appropriate dimensions, but soon enough Nieuwenhuizen would put a cross through it, or deface it with a diagonal. By some stretch of the imagination a passage would become viable, only to be obliterated a moment later by a drunken zigzag. An unmistakable corner, a perfect right angle, survived for close on an hour. Mr Malgas became convinced that it was the extremity of the rumpus room Nieuwenhuizen had once referred to. But, without blinking, Nieuwenhuizen allowed it to spin out an ugly slash that traversed the entire plan and dislocated every element of it.

"Mrs! Peanuts!"

As the geometry of string proliferated, a disturbing potential arose: with every move Nieuwenhuizen made, some portion of a new house became possible. Mr Malgas would clap his hands and give vent to his gratitude. At last, a keystone! From that he could elaborate a bathroom, say, and then a door, necessarily, and, it follows, another room . . . But sooner or later his house, rising reasonably, wall by wall, would tumble down as Nieuwenhuizen backed into it in his big boots, unreeling his string, and crossed it off the plan.

Mr Malgas was relieved when Nieuwenhuizen called it a day, and he resolved to put the plan from his mind entirely until his participation was invited once more. This looking on from the sidelines was too stressful.

The ball of string remained unbroken on the edge of the unfinished plan, wrapped in a plastic bag and weighted with stones.

"Up and down, up and down all day, busy as a butcher," Mrs told Mr the following evening when he came in from work. "Making loops and tying knots, knit one, purl one, sling two together and drop the whole caboodle."

She was ready to demonstrate the procedure with a ball of wool and some tins from the grocery cupboard, but he said gruffly, "Never mind that, I get the picture. Just tell me: Does this plan make sense? Can you see the new house? Is it taking shape?"

"Don't ask me. I'm not interested in Him and His house. I just happened to glance that way once or twice when I was making a pot of tea."

A car chase followed by a gun battle and a bomb blast, which shook the Malgases' house to its foundations, gave Nieuwenhuizen a welcome respite from prying eyes. He took what was left of the ball of string out of its protective covering, unwound the tail-end and tossed the cardboard tube into the fire on the edge of the ash-heap. It had taken him three days of back-breaking toil to finish the plan. All this movement, backwards, forwards, even sideways when necessary, had spilled ash over the secret nail. He stooped into the clearing in the ashes and blew the head clean, deposited a blob of spittle on it and polished it with his forefinger. Then he looped the remnant of string around the nail, pulled it tight and knotted the end. It fitted perfectly.

Shortly afterwards he flicked a pebble against the lounge window to attract Malgas's attention, Malgas chuffed out into the garden and they conferred through the spokes of a wagon-wheel

The plan was finished! Malgas was willing to be delighted, until he was informed that the official unveiling was scheduled for the very next day.

"Congrats!" he gulped. "I really mean it. But can't the ceremony wait for the weekend? It'll keep. Some of us have to work you know."

"Out of the question. It's now or never. You'll have to take the day off."

Malgas's mind was racing. "Mrs will give me a mouthful if I don't go to work."

"That's neither here nor there."

"In any case, I'm not ready for the plan. I won't understand it."

"There's nothing to be afraid of," Nieuwenhuizen said, reading Malgas's thoughts in the open book of his face.

While Mr was explaining why he had to take the day off, Mrs absent-mindedly picked up her china shoe, the one with the gilt buckle and the wineglass heel. She fogged the buckle with her breath and buffed it with the sleeve of her cardigan. She was about to return the shoe to its place on the mantelpiece when without warning it hiccuped and spat dust over her knuckles.

"It's an omen," she said. "We haven't had one of those for ages."

"What's it say?"

"It says you're going too far with this new house thing and one of these days you'll be sorry."

Nieuwenhuizen was waiting for Malgas at his front gate the next morning. Malgas was surprised to see him there, as he seldom – if ever – ventured beyond the borders of his own territory. Before he could remark on it ("Surprise, surprise," he was going to say) Nieuwenhuizen took him by the hand and issued instructions ("Close your eyes and shut your mouth," he said). Malgas was tingling with the novelty of playing truant and itching for an adventure. He offered his own monogrammed handkerchief (ems and aitches interwoven) as a blindfold, just to be on the safe side, but it was courteously declined. So, screwing up his eyes until they watered, he let himself be led next door, and had many little mishaps on the way, stumbled over the kerb and twisted his ankle, but not too badly, it didn't hurt any more, thanks, rubbed it vigorously and was tempted to peek, overcame temptation, stubbed his toe on a rocky outcrop there had not been reason to mention before, let alone curse to high heaven, goose-stepped over the string, felt less foolish than he might have because it was all in a good cause, was propped like an effigy in the middle of the plan.

Despite his misgivings of the night before, a spark of hope had kindled in his breast while he slept. He had woken with an inkling that the plan would be loud and clear after all and reveal the new house to him in all its splendour. Now, as his guide's footsteps receded and he waited anxiously for further instructions, with the incense of the breakfast fire in his nostrils and the morning sun inflaming his sealed eyelids, his little hope flared up into a burning desire for revelation.

From a distance, Nieuwenhuizen commanded him to see.

He opened his eyes.

All hope was snuffed out in an instant. He found himself in the midst of an immense, tattered net full of holes and knots and twisted threads, more holes than threads, as a matter of fact, but for all that utterly impenetrable. To call it a plan was to grant it a semblance of purpose and order it evidently did not deserve. It was a shambles. It was so unremittingly drunken and disorderly that tears started from Malgas's eyes.

Distantly, from the peripheries of his sight, Nieuwenhuizen invited him to explore.

Malgas remembered the web Nieuwenhuizen had woven once of transparent stuff as smooth as silk (or was it satin?) and as sweet as candy-floss. He tried to transform the bristly macramé scattered around him into that dreamy substance, but it remained stubbornly itself. Then he tried to recall the grid system, Roman numerals down one side and capitals down the other, A, I, E, A, E, E, E, but the wild and woolly scribblings made it impossible to sustain his cross-hatching. He called to mind a helpful hint: varnishes and veneers. Vrnshs 'n vnrs. Nonsense. He shifted uncomfortably from foot to foot, and the brittle crust of the earth broke into mosaic pieces and Scrabble tiles. "House," he mumbled, as if he was praying, and the verb itself shattered into spillikins against his palate.

Nieuwenhuizen's applause rang in Malgas's ears like the footfalls of a fleeing suspect.

With an effort, Malgas dragged his eyes over the plan yet again, frantic for meaning, urgently willing some fragment of the new house to rise from the jumble of nails and string. His eyes began to burn. He unpicked a thread, followed it around the perimeter of a lopsided square, lost it in a sheepshank. He picked up another, wove with it until it plunged into a knot the size of a child's fist and was gone for ever. The edges of his vision unravelled. He welcomed the onset of delusion, taking it for extra-sensory perception; and when the whole shabby web seemed to drift and billow in a troubled current, he was relieved to assume that the plan was beginning to communicate its meaning to him.

Acting on this assumption, he stepped out of the square in which he had been stranded into an adjacent triangle.

Nieuwenhuizen beamed, but Malgas was oblivious. He stepped boldly over the hypotenuse of the triangle into a rhombus. Nieuwenhuizen's face clouded over. Malgas strode across the rhombus in three long steps, gaining momentum, and jumped feet first into a rickety rectangle. The heel of his shoe caught on the dividing line and it twanged. He turned right, he stepped into a passage way segmented by countless lines of string, and hopscotched along it.

There is no telling what his next move would have been, had Nieuwenhuizen's angry cries not brought him to a sudden halt, balanced on his left foot in a small parallelogram, his right foot suspended in mid-air, like a statue of a man hopping.

Nieuwenhuizen sprang into action. He bounded onto the plan and skipped lithely from figure to figure. He made left turns, right turns, and about turns, he marched on the spot, he ran forwards, he whirled in circles and came face to face with Malgas, he seized him by the shoulders and shouted, "Where the blazes are you man? Do you have any clue?"

"Er." Malgas put down his right foot and looked wildly around. "IVG?" he asked hopelessly.

"Forgy?"

"IV-G." Malgas held up four fingers. For a delirious moment he thought he had stumbled upon the correct answer. "You know, The Grid."

"Forget about the bloody grid! We left that behind long ago. Concentrate on The Plan and tell me where you are."

Malgas chewed his cheeks.

Nieuwenhuizen rocked him backwards and forwards, and hissed, "Open your ears and I'll tell you. You're on the brink of disaster! Do you read me? One more step – just one more – and you'll plummet to a horrible end in the frog-infested moat."

Malgas tasted blood. Tears crept out of his eyes.

"There-there," Nieuwenhuizen relented, "there-there." He took Malgas gently by the arm and manoeuvred him around in a circle. "There. Can you see it now? Take your time."

"I *can't*," said Malgas in a broken voice. "We Malgases have never been good at this kind of thing."

"What you need is the guided tour," said Nieuwenhuizen. "It's a pity, I had high hopes for you once, but now it can't be helped. Wait here and keep your eyes open. And your ears." He leapt back and waved his arms around: "Observation deck!" He pointed to the left: "Balustrade." He pointed to the right: "Sliding door." He stepped over a line and pointed at the ground: "Spiral staircase." He walked downstairs and turned right: "Passage, first floor." He took five paces down the passage and his left arm shot out: "Master bedroom." His right arm shot out: "Armoury." He walked on the spot and skipped across three triangles: "Ground floor, west wing." He spun in a spiral: "Basement. Bomb shelter."

Through all this Malgas stood rooted to the spot. But now a desperate desire to participate made him tear up one heavy foot, take a ponderous step over the nearest line and say poignantly, "Guest-room."

Nieuwenhuizen flew into a towering rage. He ran furiously on the spot, turning left and right and left again, he flung his arms away and snatched them back, he went in circles and squares, he ran upstairs, he turned left, he ran up more stairs, turned right, sprinted across a landing, jumped, and shouted in Malgas's ear, "You clueless monkey! How did you get in there? Can you walk through walls? Come out at once!"

Malgas fled. Nieuwenhuizen trotted after him, shoving him in the small of his back and shouting, "You're a big waste of time, you blind buffoon. You're a stink-bomb. You'll never see the new house. Get off my plan! Off! Off!"

Mr Malgas ran into the street without looking left or right or left again. Nieuwenhuizen snapped the letter-box off its post and threw it after him. "You'll have to live in here! You're not fit to live in the new house. I don't know why I bother, really."

The letter-box clattered against the kerb.

Mr ran home, sobbing with hurt and frustration.

For hours afterwards, Nieuwenhuizen was pacing to and fro, upstairs and downstairs, from room to room, from feature to feature, naming them all to himself in a quavering voice: "Linen cupboard . . . radiogram . . . bar . . . bakelite thing . . . workshop . . . barricade, railway sleepers . . . wine-cellar . . . eye-level oven . . . dishwasher . . . working surface . . . polished polyester finish . . . burglarproofing, floral motifs . . . crazy paving . . . outdoor living area . . . moat . . . rockery . . .

gnomes . . . swimming-pool, Roman kidney . . . built-in braai-spot
. . . halogen floodlight . . . carport, double . . . servants' quarters . . .
revolving door . . . master bedroom . . . bird's-eye maple . . . Dolly
Varden . . . bathroom en suite . . . control room . . . liquor cabinet . . .
knobs . . ."

Mr looked on distraught. Mrs, still visibly shaken by her encounter with the incontinent china shoe the night before, was scrubbing
bric-à-brac in the kitchen sink. She said sharply, "It serves you right."

"It does not."

"He treats you like a dog and I'm not surprised, the way you run
after Him with your tongue hanging out. Now stop snuffling and go
to work."

At length Nieuwenhuizen arrived at, "Entrance hall . . . whatnot
. . . dimmer switch . . . front door . . . peephole . . . welcome mat . . ."
He wiped his feet, scrambled into his tent and zipped shut the flap.

Zzzzzzz.

He would not be seen again in person for several weeks.

Mr Malgas, the penitent, imagined that he had Nieuwenhuizen's skinny legs and big boots, and he took long creaking strides with these legs and bounced on his toes. He heard Nieuwenhuizen's dry bones grating together. He imagined that he had Nieuwenhuizen's thorny index finger, and he squinted down it and muttered, "Gomma Gomma armchair . . . La-Z-Boy . . . Gomma Gomma armchair . . . display cabinet . . . Gomma Gomma sofa . . . Antimacassar!"

When he started naming all the knick-knacks, in a tone of voice that seemed to mock her own cataloguing efforts, Mrs lost her temper and said, "For crying out loud, will you stop that. I can't stand it any more. If I close my eyes I could swear it's Him, right here in our midst. If you're not going to work today, why don't you make yourself useful around the home. The place is going to rack and ruin. Clean the pool. Mow the lawn. Do some weeding."

So Mr Malgas creaked around in his backyard, fingering and thumbing the rusty shafts of his neglected garden implements, and the more he tried to be like Nieuwenhuizen, the more acutely he felt his absence, and had to ache with the loss.

Poor old Malgas.

There was no sign of life at the camp. It was so quiet over there, day after day, that Mr Malgas began to suspect that Nieuwenhuizen had made good his escape under cover of darkness.

Mrs was no comfort.

"What I would like to know is this:" she said. "What does He eat? Has He been salting away songbirds and lap-dogs? Is He on some sort of starvation diet? How does He dispose of His night-soil? Does it constitute a health hazard? Does He do His ablutions in Tupperware? Can you imagine how it pongs by now in that confined space? When last did you lay eyes on Him? Yesterday? The day before? How do you know He's still in there? Does He answer when you call? What if He's made a get-away? That's all."

"He would never abandon the plan," Mr insisted. "He's not like that."

But at the end of the day he was forced to investigate and found it harrowing. His knees were shaking as he slunk along in the shadow of the hedge, averting his eyes from the plan and blocking his ears with the fleshy palms of his hands. He made a brief tour of the camp and its environs. Although the ashes in the fireplace were cold and crusted over, the gadgets were all in place, indicating that the camp was still inhabited, and heartened by this discovery he crept closer to the tent and put an ear to the canvas. Ha! He heard the stirring music of Nieuwenhuizen's breathing, in and out, round and round, like a spoon scraping the bottom of a pot.

He headed home to break the news, but got no further than the gutter, where he came across the letter-box. What a perfect symbol of his humiliation it was . . . and yet it saddened him to see it lying there, all scuffed and down at heel. He cradled it tenderly, murmured comforting words, and balanced it on top of its post.

This small constructive gesture made him feel better.

He glanced apprehensively at the plan. It was looking a little the worse for wear. He went closer. His heart began to pound again. The signs of neglect were all too clear: the string was frayed and yellowing; a nail or two had worked loose; diminutive dunes of sand and ash had rolled up around the knots. Despite the ravages of the season's bitter winds and frosts, some porraceous weeds were sprouting.

He crouched down and twirled a length of gritty string between thumb and forefinger. He became aware of Nieuwenhuizen's breathing, which rose and fell like a tide in the background, and the sound gave him goose-flesh. A salty sense of transience washed over him, dumped him head over heels in its surf, and receded, casting up this disturbing conclusion: "I, Malgas, hold the new house in my hands. In the absence of Father, who is indisposed, albeit temporarily, or is it permanent?, we don't know, I, the Malgas, am custodian of the plan, and without me it is doomed. This bewildering blueprint, bewitching too in its way, produced with faith and discipline under difficult circumstances, will fade away. The nails will rust. The string will be poached little by little to tie up packages and truss roasts and fly kites and do the million and one other indispensable, insignificant things string does. The construction site will be reclaimed by the fertile veld.

"Father has turned his back on us, it seems. But what if his heart, which is big, and strong, and soft in the middle, still cossets a spark of hope, as mine did once, even in its darkest chamber. As mine does now! What if Father emerges from his self-imposed exile – was I the sole and singular cause? I hope not – rested and restored, ready to have that spark fanned into a beacon to light our way to the future, which I see before me now, no, it's gone again – I say, emerges only to find the plan in ruins?"

Quite overcome by his own grandiloquence, Mr Malgas stumbled to the tent and called, "Daddy! Daddy!"

"Zzzzzzz." What a joker! Nieuwenhuizen had to think about his mortal remains rotting in the bowels of the earth to keep from laughing.

Mr Malgas turned back to the plan. Somehow it seemed less chaotic than before.

A voice he didn't recognize said distinctly, "Malgas."

"There must be more to life than Hardware," he made answer. "Materials are important, I won't deny it, they've been good to me. Tools too. Packaging is an art-form, the wheels must go round, these things are given. But surely one should also build, with one's own hands, according to one's own innermost desires, and be seen to build.

Ask me: I've done a bit of building in my time. Do it yourself. See our display advert."

He unbuttoned his shirt, to reveal Mr Hardware with his hammer and nail. Then he opened his eyes as wide as they'd go, walked steadfastly into the middle of the plan and chose for trial purposes an especially grubby triangle. He spat on his handkerchief and wiped the string. He dusted off a trio of nails and tightened a few knots. The improvement was dramatic. So he went back to the camp, soaked his hanky in the drum of stagnant water under the tree, wrung it out, and set about systematically cleaning the entire plan.

The following day Mr Malgas came prepared. He brought a tub of axle-grease to lubricate the shafts of the nails and safeguard them against rust, and some Silvo and a soft cloth to buff the heads. It was tricky work: he had to extract each nail from its hole, smear it and reinsert it, without undoing any knots or dropping any stitches. As if that wasn't taxing enough, no sooner had the nails been removed than the wounds would want to heal themselves. The lubrication took three days.

Next he got to work on the string, massaging the lengths with raw linseed oil and treating the knots with dubbin and beeswax. While he worked many little tasks suggested themselves, and each new one took its place in the scheme of things to constitute a routine. Some, like sweeping between the lines, he attended to daily; others, like squashing the life out of unwanted seedlings between thumb and forefinger, only when the need arose.

For three days, morning and evening, he brought food for Nieuwenhuizen and left it at the tent-flap, but it remained untouched.

"He's given up," said Mrs, "and it's the only decent thing He's done since He arrived. Why should you worry?"

"It's the least I can do. He's neglecting himself and the new house, and all because of me. If only I'd been able to see it – he wasn't asking much when you think about it – we'd have started the actual construction ages ago. We may even have been finished by now. It's all my fault. I'm a spanner in the works. It shows you how considerate he is, that he won't start without me."

"He's waiting for you because He knows you can be relied on to do the dirty work."

"What's gotten into you? Instead of carping all the time, you could help. Come over and look at the plan. You'll pick it up in no time, with your artistic streak."

"Never! What if He's creeping around and I bump into Him?"

No matter what Mrs said, Mr Malgas refused to give up. If anything, her dismissive attitude made him more determined than ever to care for the plan until Nieuwenhuizen needed it again. As the days grew longer and queued up in weeks, he refined his daily duties into a satisfying and efficient programme. As soon as he came in from work he would change into his overalls and go next door. In the unlikely event that Nieuwenhuizen had regained consciousness, he would hail him cheerfully as he approached the camp. When there was no answer, and there never was, he would cock an ear to confirm that Nieuwenhuizen was still inside the tent and breathing. This superstitious little rite never failed to lift his spirits. And only then did he bring out his maintenance kit, which he kept in a cardboard box under the hedge, and begin whatever tasks were scheduled for the day. He would be home in time to eat supper with Mrs while they watched the eight o'clock news, with special reference to the unrest report.

Initially, Mr Malgas found Nieuwenhuizen's invisible presence inhibiting. His stertorous breathing was a constant reminder of the one's confinement and the other's liberty, and insinuated a lamentable causality between the two. But he discovered ways of weaving this raucous conscience into his activities and before long he felt free to savour whole-heartedly the pleasures of caretaking. The work was absorbing. New techniques had to be devised to meet the unprecedented needs of the plan, new rhythms evolved to minimize effort and maximize effect. Concerns like these were dear to Mr Malgas. In his nurturing hands the lines became supple and beautiful again, and the nails regained their lustre. Moreover, he found that maintenance renewed his faith in the whole sphere of materials, and he began to enjoy his work in the hardware shop for the first time in months.

Mrs noticed the change in him, and cheered up as well.

In this way a semblance of normality returned to the Malgas household. It did not last.

After several weeks Mr Malgas's single-minded dedication to maintenance produced an unexpected result. One evening he was kneading a scoop of wintergreen into a fibrous knot near the heart of the plan when he noticed a breeze-block lying on the ground nearby. He looked at it in surprise, naturally, whereupon it vanished without trace.

How often in his thankless quest for the new house – at first under Nieuwenhuizen's tutelage, latterly on his own – had Malgas yearned for just such a keystone; how often had its absence weighed heavily on his mind. Yet now, when the key finally appeared, he could not grasp it! It must be a practical joke, he thought, someone's pulling my leg. But this was not borne out by the evidence. There were no mirrors to be seen, no give-away wires, no burning cigarette-ends. Nowhere on the carefully swept plot was there a single mark that Malgas could not account for, no footprint, no tell-tale gouge or scrape. Finding his way cautiously to the scene of the appearance, or rather the disappearance, as he thought of it, he went down on his hands and knees and examined the surface closely, but the breeze-block itself had left no impression. He was forced to dismiss it as a figment of his imagination, a side-effect of stress and overwork. Wasn't he holding down two jobs? He didn't breathe a word to Mrs.

The following evening's shift held no surprises. But the day after was a Saturday, and he was obliged to spend the whole afternoon tending the plan. Towards sunset he was sweeping with a grass broom when a ghostly balustrade floated into view some five metres above the ground and dependent upon nothing at all.

A less steadfast man might have taken to his heels, but Malgas stood firm. He even had the presence of mind not to confront the apparition directly. He sensed danger: he saw himself turned to stone. So he maintained the steady rhythm of his sweeping and watched the floating balustrade out of the corner of his eye. It shimmered, and shimmied, and emitted a halo of brilliant light. It faded, and was on the point of vanishing altogether, but, as Malgas's heart skipped a beat, it glowed again with new intensity and appeared to stabilize and solidify somewhat. It grew a landing, it excreted a film of crimson linoleum, it oozed wax. Then it gave birth to a flight of stairs, each riser condensing in the incandescent vapour and toppling in slow motion from the edge of the tread above it, shuffling languidly into place. The handrails of the grand staircase curved gracefully, uncoiling like stems, and progressed slowly but surely down to the ground. A pool of yellow light seeped out, gathered itself, and extruded from its syrupy depths five strips of Oregon pine, which hovered just above the surface. They came closer, he smelt wax and sawdust, they eased in below the speeding bristles of his broom. The bristles chased over the floorboards and scared clouds of lemon-scented dust out of the cracks. These particles spun gaily in the rosy air, phosphoresced into pointy golden stars and sifted gently down, enveloping him.

Malgas let out his breath with a whoosh. He cast aside his broom, dispersing the staircase into a haze of ordinary dust-motes, and launched himself across the plan in an ecstasy, whooping with joy and bellowing to wake the dead, "I can see! I can see!"

Nieuwenhuizen slept through the ruckus, but Mrs came running to the lounge window and looked on aghast.

Round and round went Mr, leaping into the air and waving his fists, drumming on his thighs, tearing his hair, laughing and crying, smearing his tears into mud on his cheeks, frothing at the mouth, rolling head over heels, swallowing his tongue, collapsing, steaming. Yes.

"I've tried to be happy for you," Mrs said, "but I really don't get this. Are you imagining things? Is it a case of play-play? Are you hallucinating? What the hell's going on out there?"

"None of the above," Mr replied firmly. "The new house . . . *materializes.* It's a manifestation."

"He's having visions."

"Of course, one has to be receptive."

"Goes without saying."

"Then it's like this – although words don't do it justice: a paintbrush with a tousled head swooshes across a blank screen, and swooshes back again, scattering gold-dust and glitter, and 1-2-3, a multi-storey mansion appears, in full colour."

"As if by magic?"

"Hey presto! Clinker brick and corrugated iron."

She thought: He's flipped his lid, he's seeing things. But I suppose we should count our blessings. At least it's all in his mind; the real thing would be intolerable.

Now that he had something concrete to go on, Malgas tried to engage Nieuwenhuizen in conversation, on the reasonable assumption that a familiar voice and a well-loved topic would coax him back into the land of the living, and so he introduced a daily report-back into his programme. During these sessions he sat on a stone at the end of the tent where he imagined Nieuwenhuizen's head to be and spoke matter of factly about his new powers of insight. "I must say: Bakelite, yes," he would say, "balusters, bay windows, breastsummers, bricks of course, and, I almost forgot, braai-spots. Please insert, I do declare."

Then he tended the plan, and block by block, wall by wall, with an unpredictable oozing of mortar and PVA, with innumerable proliferations and ramifications, with digressions, diversions and divagations, with false starts, blind spots and dead ends, with set-backs and quantum leaps, two steps forward and one step back, the new house made an appearance, until one day he found himself enclosed in it, surrounded on all sides and sealed off from the outside world. And still the house continued to grow: here a room, there a room, here a passage in between. Here a wall, there a wall, here a screen. And storey by storey, here a floor, there a floor, now a mezzanine, the house continued to grow.

It was a magnificent place, every bit as grand as Malgas had thought it would be, but it had its shortcomings, which he was quick to perceive too. It had no depth. It had the deceptive solidity of a stage-set. The colours were unnaturally intense, yet at the slightest lapse of concentration on his part the whole edifice would blanch and sway as if it was about to fall to pieces.

"It has to be said," he said, feeling insecure.

Interestingly, although he had learned to see the new house, and understood that this accomplishment was somehow connected with his love for the plan, the exact relationship between the two continued to elude him. He was puzzling over this one day when he recalled the secret nail, which had lain forgotten under the compacted remains of the ash-heap. No sooner had he called the nail to mind, than the entire house spurted out of the ground.

Until this moment he had never dared to venture from his post in the entrance hall at the foot of the grand staircase, but now he was carried aloft on a wave of optimism and found himself in a reception room on the second floor with the whole house humming around him, alive to his senses, ablaze with light and colour. As he gazed upon his luscious surroundings, his mouth began to water. The place was good enough to eat. He would start on the wall next to the fireplace – layers of flaky stone sandwiching globs of caramelized mortar, studded with cherries and nuts. He had never seen so much light gathered together in one place! It poured from crystal chandeliers and twisty candelabra. It dripped from lozenges of coloured glass. It seeped like honey from the brick and gleamed like a sugared glaze on slabs of creamy marble and chocolaty wood.

It was so sweet to be alive inside the new house that Malgas swooned.

Everything fell into place.

The secret nail, pulsing like a beacon, drew Malgas to a room under the stairs which had been set aside especially for him. It was musty and narrow, and the ceiling sloped awkwardly and made him stoop, but a bright rug and a swinging lantern made it cosy as a casket. There was a hammock, and an armchair with a soft cushion for the small of the back, a side-table with a reading-lamp, and a toolbox that doubled as a footstool.

When Mr told Mrs about his room she sniffed and said, "I always knew you'd want to go off without me some day."

Practice makes perfect, and Malgas was something of a perfectionist. He practised seeing the new house until it came out of his ears. He popped open its rooms as if they were Chinese lanterns and stretched out entire wings like concertinas. He telescoped columns and slotted them into moist sockets on balconies. He unrolled floors and stacked up stairs. He rollercoastered reams of tiles over the rafters.

Then, in the wink of an eye, he did all of these things again in reverse.

He also practised being in the new house. He practised strolling around in the rooms and leaning in the interleading doorways. He went into every room at least once, not excepting the tiniest ante-chamber or alcove. When he knew where everything was, he practised the everyday tasks that would transform the house, in time, into a home: ringing the bell, locking the security gate, listening to messages on the answering-machine, filling the kettle, turning on the telly, sitting on the couch, eating the TV dinner, answering the telephone, Hello?, straightening the pictures, leafing through the magazines, sighing, putting out the cat, filling the hot-water bottle, switching on the bedside lamp, turning back the corner of the carpet, picking up the paper-knife. When he had finished practising for the day, he rested in his room under the stairs.

It was during one of these rest periods that Nieuwenhuizen reappeared on the scene.

"There you are," he said from the doorway, into which he had slotted himself without making the slightest sound, "I've been looking for you everywhere."

Malgas was astonished at the sight of him. His cheeks were like crumpled wrapping-paper. A child had coloured his features in with thick wax-crayons – purple for the lips, bottle-green for the nose, blood-red for the eyes. The hair on his head was scribbled Indian ink. Under lids like wads of damp blotting-paper his irises spluttered fitfully. Malgas was filled with pity and compassion for the owner of this vandalized face; but he knew that restraint was called for, so he kept his emotions in check, continued to dandle himself in his hammock, and said simply, "Here I am."

"You've made yourself at home."

"I've been seeing to things in your absence. Everything's here, in perfect shape."

"My faithful Malgas. I'm proud of you."

This tribute moved Malgas deeply. It seemed to him that the time had now come to express his feelings. "I think we've both been marvellous," he said, lumbering to his feet and embracing Nieuwenhuizen. His confinement had left him thinner and drier than ever: he felt like a bundle of reeds. When Malgas released him he staggered back and blinked his droopy eyes. "It's bright in here."

Malgas averted the reading-lamp, suddenly ashamed of his own tears, and said bluffly, "Can I get you something? Juice? Lager?"

"It's cold for beer. But a whisky would hit the spot."

"Let's make our way then to the built-in bar."

Malgas bustled Nieuwenhuizen out of the doorway, pulled the door shut and took him by his sharp elbow. They walked. When Malgas heard the tentative *squee? squee?* of Nieuwenhuizen's rubber soles and the affirmative patter of his own velskoene, the turmoil in his heart subsided and he began to recover his composure. They went upstairs and passed down a long, gleaming gallery. At the end they turned right and elbowed through batwing doors into the bar. Nieuwenhuizen sat on a tall stool, which had brass trimmings and was bolted to the floor, while Malgas mixed the drinks.

Then side by side, with glasses in hand, Nieuwenhuizen, on the left, and Malgas, on the right, walked through the new house.

At the end of every sparkling corridor they saw their own reflections in full-length mirrors and polished stone, in smoked-glass partitions and lacquered panels, and all these silent witnesses to their containment conspired to give Malgas the courage of his convictions.

In one of the guest-rooms a log was burning in an ornate fireplace and they stopped to warm their hands. Malgas gave the fender a smart kick. "White Sicilian marble," he murmured, as if to himself, "and beige sandstone shot through with lilac."

"Decorative mouldings in the traditional style, riddled with character," Nieuwenhuizen assented in a whisper. "Fluted pilasters and hand-carved rosettes. Tuffaceous blocks?"

They drew closer together and went on, in a rosier light and a more companionable silence, which their muted conversation served only to enhance.

"Light fittings."

"Rise and fall shades . . ."

". . . with bobble fringes."

Their words shuttled between them, binding them temple to temple in a soft shell of naming.

"Occasional chairs."

"Diamond-padded backs . . ."

". . . in ruby dralon."

"Swags and festoons."

"Alabaster plinths . . ."

". . . and plastic dados."

"Occasional tables."

"Dappled sunlight . . ."

". . . on melamine."

Later, Nieuwenhuizen dozed off in the library with a dusty old volume on his lap, and Malgas tiptoed out onto the observation deck for a breath of fresh air.

It was a glorious night. The moonlight gleamed like lengths of chrome-plated beading on the balusters and telescopes. The moat was a mass of silvery brushmarks. Nieuwenhuizen's camp, tucked away in a corner of the yard near the servants' quarters, with all its quaint equipment scattered about, looked small and remote. Malgas had never seen a more beautiful sight; his heart overflowed with wonder and gratitude.

"We'll have a garden too," he said to himself, surveying the barren soil, "with patios and grottos, red-hot pokers and bottle-brushes, tennis-courts and hiking trails, an aviary and a fishpond with a wooden bridge going over. But we'll keep the camp just as it is, for the generations who come after us. We'll declare it a monument, an open-air museum. We'll never forget where we came from."

Then Malgas wished that he could gaze down upon his own house as well and make some comment about it, but it was nowhere to be seen.

He went inside. Nieuwenhuizen was still slumped in a wicker chair drawn up to the fire. The familiar cadence of his snoring moved Malgas anew. He touched the hem of Nieuwenhuizen's safari suit, as if to assure himself that he was real, and said softly, "Father?"

Nieuwenhuizen woke up with a start, his book fell face-down on the carpet, he sneezed and said, "Please, you must call me Otto."

"Bless you! Pardon?"

"Otto."

"Ot-to?"

"*Otto.*"

"Ot-to." The name snapped in Malgas's mouth. He swallowed one piece gamely, tucked the other into his cheek with his tongue, and went on, "Do you mind if I make an observation at this point in time?"

"So long as it's brief. Sometimes you're like a bloody broken record."

Malgas swallowed again. "I would just like to say that if it wasn't for you, I wouldn't be standing here today."

"Ditto. Do you play chess?"

"No . . . In the early days I played a little checkers . . ."

"Rummy? Good. There's a deck of cards in the rumpus room."

Nieuwenhuizen led the way there. Malgas walked behind, looking at the back of Nieuwenhuizen's scruffy head as if he was seeing it for the first time, and saying "Otto" to himself shyly.

After just one game, which he won, Nieuwenhuizen said, "It's been a long day, I'm falling asleep on my feet." Malgas thought that an invitation to stay over would follow, but Nieuwenhuizen added, "I'll walk you to the door."

On the doorstep they shook hands, although Malgas would have preferred a manly embrace.

"Beautiful place you've got here, Otto." He managed to get it out in one piece. "Sleep well."

"Cheerio." The door clicked shut.

For a long time Malgas stood on the welcome mat, stamping his feet and rubbing his hands together, and hearing again and again the key grating in the lock and the tumblers tumbling. This signalled some new phase of his life, of that he was sure, and finally it came to him: companionship.

He looked at the doorbell and the burnished knocker. He listened to Nieuwenhuizen banging around upstairs, closing windows and drawing curtains. He heard him going from room to room, he heard him coming downstairs. Surely he would sleep in the master bedroom? He felt him stooping into the room under the stairs.

"My room!"

Malgas was beside himself.

"He's paying tribute to me again. No, it's more than that: It's an act of solidarity!"

This possibility was so distracting that the new house faded away in an instant. The plan was revealed, and so was Nieuwenhuizen, snuggling down in the ash heap.

"Otto?"

Mrs opened a drawer in her dressing-table and found that it was full of sand.

"It's Him. It's come to pass: He's everywhere. It's not healthy to be near Him, to breathe His emanations, but you can't help it."

The contagion settled thickly on armrests and working surfaces. No amount of dusting would drive it away. Mrs gave up. She lay on her bed with a scarf soaked in Dettol and almond essence tied over her face. She listened to her knick-knacks jumbling themselves up in the cabinets. When the din became unbearable she dragged herself to the lounge to watch television. It was cold comfort, but she persevered with a melancholic submissiveness.

The box brought nothing but unrest and disorder, faction fights and massacres, even blood-baths, high-pressure systems and cold fronts, situation comedies and real-life dramas, hijackings, coups, interviews with VIPs, royal weddings, exposés, scandals, scoops, conspicuous consumptions, white-collar crimes, blue-collar detergents, epidemics, economic indicators, peace talks, heart-warming instances of bravery and kindness to strangers, advertisements for dogfood and requests for donations. Each new atrocity struck Mrs like a blow, and she thrashed about in the La-Z-Boy like a political prisoner.

Malgas took two instant dinners in crimped aluminium containers from the deep-freeze and arranged them, with sprigs of parsley, on a plastic tray depicting the Last Supper in three dimensions. He carried the tray through to the library. Nieuwenhuizen was gazing into the flames, a dog-eared old volume open on his knees, forgotten. Malgas displayed the dinners and said, "What's it to be tonight?"

"What's the difference?" Nieuwenhuizen barely glanced at the offering.

"This is a trout," Malgas said patiently, "and this is a cottage pie." The names of the dishes were in fact printed in violet letters on the cardboard lids.

Nieuwenhuizen waved a dismissive hand.

"The trout has been deboned," Malgas persisted, "and stuffed with shredded spinach and chopped walnuts, flavoured subtly with marjoram butter, freshly ground pepper and a squeeze of lemon. Essential mnrls and vtmns – are you with me? – 30% of the RDA. The cottage pie is more basic."

"You choose."

"The cottage pie is also known as a shepherd's pie, for some reason now lost to us. It consists of minced meat baked under a shroud of mashed potatoes. Or it will when I've put it in the microwave."

"I don't care. Just do it."

"I know! It was made with mutton, once upon a time, sheep would die of exposure, bad shepherds, and potatoes are cheap and freely available."

Nieuwenhuizen burst from his chair like a jack-in the-box and writhed out of the room. The old volume, launched carelessly from his lap, flapped through the air and crash-landed in the fire. Malgas leapt to the rescue with the tongs, then thought better of it and left it to burn.

"I'll bake you both and we'll go halves," he said to the dinners and hurried them back to the kitchen.

Mr Malgas stopped going to work. He lost weight and he began to smell, because he wouldn't eat and he wouldn't bath. All he would do was keep Nieuwenhuizen company.

And Mrs, despite her better intentions, found that she could do nothing but observe. Her loneliness and lack of self-esteem pressed in upon her and her health declined. She wasn't allowed to do the ironing anymore. She wouldn't dust. The Hoover had given up the ghost. Day after day, week after week, she had to watch them going through the motions.

On a typical morning Mr went next door at dawn. He looked in the letter-box. BEWARE OF THE DOG! He marched boldly towards the plan, which sad to say was now a pale and tatty shadow of its former self, and stepped into it. He waved his hands around, shuffled sideways, walked, knocked, buzzed, tweaked, fiddled with the air, opened it and went inside.

"Otto!"

"Cooee!"

"Cookalooks!" Mrs cried, and bit her tongue so hard it bled.

Nieuwenhuizen turned over in the ashes, stretched, rose, opened the door under the stairs and shook Mr's hand. Side by side they began to walk. They walked up and down and on the spot. They went in circles and seated themselves on the ground. They spoke briefly. Three times Nieuwenhuizen got to his feet, threw himself into the air, and allowed his limbs to rattle down like pick-up sticks. Mr followed his example, laughing good-naturedly even while he was bruising himself and spraining various parts of his body.

Then Nieuwenhuizen excused himself and sloped away to a corner of the plan, where he leant on the air and stared into space. Mr took off his clothes. He rubbed sand and ash all over his skin and scraped it off with sticks and stones. He danced around. He put on his clothes again and went and stood next to Nieuwenhuizen, staring out. They walked together, arm in arm, and stopped, walked apart and waved to each other, lay down on the ground like a pair of brackets, and went to sleep.

Malgas dreamt that he and Nieuwenhuizen were flying at a great height (side by side).

When they awoke they sat together again in a triangle of string, like toddlers in a play-pen, staring and talking. Then they stood up, patted themselves, and walked all over the show, each according to his own inclinations, careful to avoid the camp, going in circles, hopping, turning left and right, until they were reunited at the front door, whereupon they shook hands and shouted out greetings.

"Farewell!"

"Sweet dreams!"

Mr stepped out of the plan and walked to the street. He looked in the letter-box and came home.

"Your food's in the warming-drawer," Mrs said. "Probably spoilt."

"I'm not hungry," said Mr with a wan smile. "I couldn't eat a horse. Not even a pony."

"You should put something in your stomach. Your clothes are hanging on you."

"I've eaten."

"You look like death warmed up," she said, trying to wipe the smile off his face, "and you smell like bonemeal. We'll be digging you into the flower-beds one of these fine days. For the phlox."

But Mr was too happy for words. He drifted through his house as if it wasn't there. He lay down in a dark corner of the pantry and fell asleep with a smile on his lips.

Mrs wanted to describe what he'd been up to, but she couldn't get a word in edgeways.

.   .   .

On an evening like this, a fairly typical evening when all is said and done, as Mrs Malgas lay alone in the clutches of the La-Z-Boy, the unrest report finally delivered up, as an item of news, the film of a woman being burnt alive.

A woman suspected of being a spy, the unrest reporter declared, was set alight today by an angry mob.

There was a warning that sensitive viewers might find the following scenes distressing, and Mrs shut her eyes responsibly. But when the screen cast its light upon her lids, it came to her that she had been waiting for nothing so much as this moment, and she felt obliged to open her eyes again, and saw the burning woman running down a road between matchbox houses.

A burning woman!

A woman suspected of being a spy.

I spy something beginning with a B. A burning.

The people who had set the woman alight, beginning with an L, the one who had struck the match and the curious others drawn to the flames, and furious others afraid of the dark, ran after the woman and breathed the smoke. She leapt into the air. One of her shoes flew off. She fell and crumpled into a ball, and her tattered red frock settled over her. The others, delirious fools, appalled arrangements of dots, gathered and by their watching fuelled, the woman curled, the woman unfurled and stood up again on two legs. A shoe.

Brth.

A woman on fire! Aflame.

The moths, ordinary people, the other poor mirrors, momentarily scattered, gathered again. Mrs found herself in the smothering circle of onlookers, scattering and gathering, gazing upon, pull yourself together, their illuminated faces, as if, as if the naming of their expressions, by the light of the human torch, by its dying, its death, were the claiming of her own.

She switched off the set, belatedly, and the image died down into two coals under her eyelids. Remembers, embers, mbrs, mrs, s.

Mrs thought about the fact that she was sensitive. Was documentary proof required? Written evidence?

Then Mrs thought about Mr and how he was embarrassing himself. He was up to maggots and losing weight – even the spare tyre. His happiness was consuming him. And Nieuwenhuizen? There were bits and pieces of Him everywhere. What was left of Him? She rose and went towards the window, but the net curtain blew like smoke into her face and she was turned back gasping into her restless household.

Nieuwenhuizen and Malgas sat down to pass the time of day in their easy chairs in the rumpus room. They had spent an active morning playing a version of snap thought up by Malgas, involving fixtures and features, and they were both pleasantly tuckered out.

They mulled over a comfortable silence.

Malgas looked once again at the bandoleer and the hunter's hat, which Nieuwenhuizen had taken to wearing day and night. Malgas had always disapproved of the bandoleer, although it may have suited the rough and ready atmosphere of the camp. But in the new house it was totally out of place. As for the hat . . . did one really need protective headgear indoors? Had it come to that? He'd been meaning to say something all day, but held back for fear of spoiling the easy comradeship that had developed between them. Perhaps criticism was premature? Time had to pass, it had to be allowed to pass unmolested.

Or had the right moment arrived? Did the moment have to be challenged with an unpronounceable password? He formulated a question, edited it, and was about to come out with it when Nieuwenhuizen raised his right hand to hush him, kinked his eyebrows into kappies (circumflexes) and formed a perfect O with his lips, flexed his fingers, plunged his hand like a grapnel through the floorboards, fished, and hauled up a section of the plan.

Malgas couldn't believe his eyes. He gazed in horror at the splintered boards and the string purling from the hole like a distended vein. Nieuwenhuizen stretched the string over his knuckles and snapped it. Both ends burst into tufts of throbbing fibres. He pinned one of the loose ends under an elephant-foot pouffe; he wound the other tightly around his fist and stood up. Not a moment too soon either, for the empty chair sank to its haunches even as he rose. He backed across the room, pulling the string up through the floor as he went. It sliced through the varnished pine like a knife through buttered gingerbread.

The house shivered.

Nieuwenhuizen disappeared through a doorway into the next room, coiling the plan on his left arm between thumb and elbow. Malgas stumbled after him, croaking and gesturing at the crumbly edges of the gash. His knees were shaking, and his hands were opening and closing on the air.

There was a fireplace in this room, which was a reception room of some description, there was a fire in the grate, and Nieuwenhuizen bore down on it unerringly. He reached into the flames, smashing the hearthstone to smithereens, and jerked up a nail in a tangle of string. He extricated the nail, wiped some sticky flames off it on his thigh, puffed the heat out of it and pushed it through a loop in the bandoleer. It fitted.

Malgas found his voice, but now he couldn't find anything to say with it. He hopped backwards and forwards over the gash and felt the house trembling as the shock set in. At last a sentence came to him – it wasn't quite right but it would have to suffice – and he steeled himself and declaimed: "In the name of decency, stop this senseless destruction!"

Nieuwenhuizen glanced at him quizzically, snorted, picked a new thread out of the ashes in the broken hearth and walked through a wall, shattering masonry and woodwork. Malgas heard him in the next room, coughing and laughing. He made to follow him through the jagged hole, in which a storm of plaster dust and wood shavings still raged – but he couldn't bring himself to do it. He'd have to take the long way round. He ran out into the passage and plotted Nieuwenhuizen's position as he went. I.

Nieuwenhuizen had come out in an unused *en suite* bathroom in the east wing. When Malgas caught up with him, he was standing coyly in the broken shell of the bathtub disengaging his nails from the plan, which had frothed into a clot on his left arm, and loading the bandoleer. He was powder-white and there were crumbs of brick and flakes of ceramic tile on the brim of his hat. A severed pipe gushed soapy water over his boots. He stepped out of the bath ever so daintily, flattened a screen and emerged in the bedroom. He began reeling in handfuls of string from under the bed.

Desperate measures were called for. Malgas filled his lungs with abrasive air and said, "What's going on here Father – I mean Otto?"

"I'm getting rid of this old thing."

"This 'old thing' is our beloved plan, the apple of our eye. Do I have to remind you?"

"It's fucked."

"What!"

"Excuse my French. It's had it. Kaput."

"You haven't consulted me. We can sit down and talk it over, by all means, I don't even mind if we stand, but I must be consulted before the fact. I think you owe me an explanation for this unaccountable behaviour."

"I don't owe you anything, let's face it. But if it gets your goat – and I can see it does, don't ask me why – I can explain. It's simple: the plan has served its purpose. We have no more use for it. Don't just stand there, give me a hand with it. The sooner this is all over, the better."

Nieuwenhuizen tugged at the ball of string and a volley of nails tore through the carpet in a cloud of desiccated underfelt. The room shuddered as if someone had walked over its grave. A crack ran opportunely through a wall. Malgas braced himself in the door-case; Nieuwenhuizen, by comparison, sat down on the bed to undo a knot. The wall behind him swayed, and a picture-rail and two landscapes in ornate gilt frames broke loose from it and floated down to the floor. They smashed spectacularly, with no sound effects, and a wave of fragments cascaded into the room, sluiced off Nieuwenhuizen's hat and shoulders, and, subsiding, poured between Malgas's legs. Malgas fell on his knees and cupped his palms for the bobbing pieces, but they drained away into the swamp.

"Please stop!" Malgas gurgled, losing all self-respect. "I still need the plan. I won't be able to see without it. I'll go under."

But Nieuwenhuizen was firm. "I'm sorry, it has to go. They're bringing my stuff at four o'clock and I've got to be finished by then. I can't keep them waiting. In any case, this place is a death-trap. Someone's bound to trip and break something."

"What stuff?"

"My goods."

Malgas grovelled in his failure to understand.

"My furniture," Nieuwenhuizen said in an exasperated, parental tone.

"You never said you had *furniture* . . ."

"Of course I've got furniture! Use your head: a man of my age."

"Well, let's say you've got it, but we won't be needing it. Why not? you interject. It's obvious, I retort with finality: We've already got furniture. We don't have space for more."

"I'll be the judge of that."

"It's not right." Malgas was close to tears. "I won't let you do it, we've been through too much together."

"Who the hell do you think you are?" Nieuwenhuizen said angrily. "The architect? The landlord?"

Malgas sniffed and looked at his hands.

"This is my house," Nieuwenhuizen went on. "My namesake. You're just a visitor . . . not even that, some sort of janitor – a junior one, with no qualifications and precious little experience, and damned lucky to have a broom cupboard all to yourself. What were you when I discovered you and took an interest in your welfare? A DIY good-for-nothing, that's what, a tongue-tied nobody. What I say around here goes, is that clear? Look at me when I'm talking to you. Crumbs! To think that you'd turn on me like this, after all I've done for you. It hurts me, it really does."

With that Nieuwenhuizen swung on his heel, bundling up nails and string in his arms, and walked through the cracked wall. He passed through an eye-level oven and a kitchen sink, upsetting a half-baked bread and butter pudding and a stack of dirty dishes in the process, and came out in the walk-in cupboard in the master bedroom. He walked out of that, he slid through two walls, he sank through a floor and stood in Malgas's room under the stairs with his head jutting through the ceiling.

Malgas jumped up and ran after him, choking in the confetti that gusted in his wake. Malgas took the long way round; Nieuwenhuizen took the short cuts. Malgas glimpsed him at the end of corridors, through archways and serving-hatches, moving fearlessly through space. At each new breach of its integrity, the house trembled more violently.

In his hurried descent of the grand staircase Malgas nearly tripped over Nieuwenhuizen's head, resting like an over-dressed coconut against one of the risers. He hurdled over it to the foot of the stairs and snatched open the door to his room. He found Nieuwenhuizen standing to attention on the rug, with his heels together and his toes apart. The space between his boots was an arrowhead that pointed precisely at the secret nail, nestling in the darkness below the floorboards. Flaccid lengths of string straggled from holes in the rug and led to the bundle of plan which swung nonchalantly in the hammock.

In a flash Malgas understood Nieuwenhuizen's intention, but it was too late to stay his hand. Nieuwenhuizen reached down through the rug and seized the plan where it was secured to the secret nail. Sawdust and ash squirted up through the rents. He tugged. The nail held – but only for a moment. Then it shot out into the light with a screech that drowned out Malgas's own cry of pain. The secret nail, secret no more, in an instant made unpardonably public, dangled in a cat's cradle of string. It flew this way and that for no apparent reason. It was cold and grey. All the fire had gone out of it.

The house grew pale. Malgas saw right through it, from one end to the other. He saw tumblers tumbling idly in locks, he saw doors opening and closing in endless succession, he saw filaments in lightbulbs crumpling into squiggles of ash, he saw the head of a match exploding. As a result he began to cry, and he called out pathetically, "The house! The house!"

"Stop that."

"The house. It's falling down around our ears."

"Oh don't be such a cry-baby. If I'd known you'd behave like this I never would have let you in."

"All my hard work for nothing," Malgas sobbed. "I had it by heart, and now you're breaking it down."

"It's not in the heart, you clot, it's in the head." Nieuwenhuizen tipped back his hat so that Malgas could see the bulge of his forehead. "This clinging to one thing is unseemly in a breadwinner. What's in a house? There's plenty more where this one came from."

As he spoke he rifled a Moorish townhouse complex from his hatband, balanced it in his palm, scrunched it up, popped it into his mouth and swallowed it. He opened his mouth wide to show that it was indeed empty. This captured Malgas's attention: he stared at the breakwater of yellow teeth and the pink tongue lapping against them. Now Nieuwenhuizen flourished his hand and one after the other half a dozen modest family homes blossomed between his fingers, rolled over his knuckles and vanished.

Malgas took a wad of cotton waste out of his sleeve and blew his nose.

"That's better."

To crown it all, Nieuwenhuizen plucked a mansion from behind Malgas's ear. It was a cute miniature, complete with towers and battlements, a double garage and a carport, a flagpole and a drawbridge, a fibreglass swimming-pool with a Slasto surround and a Kreepy Krauly, a diving-board, a jungle gym and a putt-putt course. It was so much like the new house, which even then was creaking and swaying all around them, and so hopelessly out of proportion, that Malgas felt a sludge of inconsolable grief welling up in his chest. He would have burst out crying again, but Nieuwenhuizen tossed the little house up into the air, where it self-destructed with a thunderclap, and said cheerfully, "See? There's no point in getting sentimental. Now give me a hand with this plan."

"It's all over," Malgas thought. He felt tired and empty. He began to help Nieuwenhuizen with his unenviable task. Someone had to do it. Nieuwenhuizen discarded the bandoleer: he said they had lost too much time in pointless discussion to bother with salvaging the nails, so they rolled the string up nails and all. Malgas took no pleasure in this little victory.

As the plan came up, the house shivered convulsively and grew transparent; roof-tiles and chimney pots clattered down over the gutters and plunged into the still waters of the moat; chunks of masonry cracked out of the walls and bounced across the floors like painted polystyrene.

Malgas tried not to look at the splintered boards and crumbling walls, or at Nieuwenhuizen's clumsy boots and the crosses and arrows they were imprinting in drifts of sawdust and icing sugar. He held the familiar shapes of the rooms in his palms and tried to keep the new house whole, even though his heart was no longer in it.

At four o'clock, true to Nieuwenhuizen's word, a delivery van bearing his goods drew up outside. The van was green, and on its side was a golden gonfalon held up by manikins in overalls, identical twins, and on the gonfalon were the words SPEEDY REMOVALS. You could tell by the hundreds of tapering brush-marks blurring their outlines what a hurry the little men were in.

Malgas was sitting on the doorstep with his head in his hands. Nieuwenhuizen perched on the edge of the stoep, resting his feet on the hobnailed lump which was all that remained of the plan. They had nothing to say to one another, although Nieuwenhuizen's bobbing head spoke volumes. Two removers – the driver and an assistant – alighted from the cab and Nieuwenhuizen went to confer with them, shaking each one's hand in turn and chatting away quite naturally, giving and taking counsel. Malgas was relieved to see that there were only two. There didn't seem to be much furniture either, although what there was looked old and ugly. A lounge suite, a wardrobe, a chest of drawers; standing lamps and plants in pots; white goods. A dozen cardboard boxes. Malgas examined the boxes critically and found them wanting: second-rate materials, shoddily folded and half-heartedly sealed. The signs saying THIS SIDE UP were all upside-down.

Under Nieuwenhuizen's direction the removers unloaded a settee from the van and carried it to the house. Malgas scrambled out of their way and inspected this item as it sailed past him. It was made of a dark and grainy wood, thickly varnished, barnacled with bubble gum and scratched by countless fingernails, knitting-needles and keys, branded by who knew what cigarette-ends and coffee mugs. It had muscular cabriole legs with ball and claw feet, but its arms were sadly wasted and terminated in arthritic talons. The stuffing was foaming out of the cushions, and springs spiralled out of the brocade. The removers, by contrast, were neatly dressed in spanking new tartan caps (in grass-green and lemon) and green overalls of a leafier shade with knife-edge creases in the legs and old-gold piping on the cuffs and turn-ups.

"Coincidence?" Malgas wanted to know.

In lieu of an answer Nieuwenhuizen walked through the front door without bothering to open it. The removers, clutching the settee like a battering-ram, stomped after him and smashed the door off its hinges. When Malgas saw these rude, unthinking strangers trampling the welcome mat underfoot and barging into the new house without even knocking or doffing their caps, his blood ran cold. Nieuwenhuizen rushed ahead, waving his arms flamboyantly, and the removers hurried after him, bashing down walls and uprooting fittings.

While they went in circles, looking for a place to put the settee down, Malgas stood on the grand staircase possessed by a glorious will to self-sacrifice. His eyes were popping, his throat was burning, his brow was baubled with lymph. Then his soles began to smoulder and he sank up to his knees through the boards. He was almost overcome. But in the nick of time a desperate will to self-preservation repossessed him and tumbled him headlong down the stairs. This dramatic re-entry went unnoticed by Nieuwenhuizen and his cohorts.

The removers brought in heaps of goods. Nieuwenhuizen flung himself around like a rag doll, inciting them to more and more reckless antics. They began to prance and pirouette in their camouflaged tackies, whirling the furnishings through space and weaving after them. They laughed uproariously, and whispered loudly when Nieuwenhuizen's back was turned, and every time something came apart at the seams or fell into holes or went to pieces they threw their caps into the air and punched one another's shoulders. They took no notice of Malgas at all. He was invisible.

For an hour on end Malgas dodged around them like a presentiment, opening doors and windows, moving ornaments and artefacts out of harm's way, even going so far as to place his own soft body between the blunt instrument and the object of his affection. But all these efforts were in vain.

In the inevitable end, Nieuwenhuizen and the removers whipped themselves up into a cloud of dust and typography, and Malgas could no more marshal them than you or I. The cloud boiled and spilled out fists and feet, caps and hats, asterisks and ampersands, dollar signs and percentages, sharps and flats, ›, ‹, and =. Malgas submitted. He flopped down in an emaciated armchair. His hair was full of glass. His mouth was full of dust. His heart was out of order.

"On your feet, Lazy-bones!" Nieuwenhuizen cried, popping out of the mêlée all stuck with quotation marks and iron filings. He kicked the sole of Malgas's shoe and beckoned him to follow.

Malgas walked behind Nieuwenhuizen to the van. It was a relief to be out in the still air, in the moonlight. He looked back at the house as they walked: he could see the ribs of the rafters through the tiles. Now, more than ever, he wanted to say a few words, but his mind was a riot of capital letters and punctuation which his tongue could not manage. Nieuwenhuizen whistled a song and skipped, but he too said nothing.

They unloaded a freezer, carried it around to the east wing and squelched through the bottom of the moat. A fish out of water applauded flippantly. In a fit of abnegation Malgas steered them through a sliding door and smashed it into a pool of troubled light. He ground the sugary pieces with his heels; he dropped his end of the freezer on a teapoy; he kicked a terracotta statuette into the air. Nieuwenhuizen ignored all these attempts to communicate.

The house reeled around them, but it refused to fall. Malgas could only wonder at the obstinacy that kept it standing even as its chambers filled up with gloom.

Nieuwenhuizen became a child. He ripped open the cardboard boxes gleefully, and his playmates began to scatter his household effects in the topsy-turvy rooms. They propped pictures against the walls and lobbed ornaments onto ledges. They rolled his threadbare rugs over the floors. They piled his copper-bottomed pots and pans in leaning towers and shied them with shoes and table-legs. They threw toilet-rolls like streamers, and handfuls of pills and charcoal briquettes.

When they were finished Nieuwenhuizen gave them money, whisky and cardboard boxes, and they knocked off for the day and went to their van to relax.

Nieuwenhuizen himself prepared to go back to the camp. Before he left he took Malgas aside and said, "Mal, I've had a ball here today. I hope you have too."

Malgas opened his mouth but no sound came out.

"What's the matter with you?" Nieuwenhuizen asked. "Is your nose still out of joint?"

Malgas put a finger on Nieuwenhuizen's lips to hush him and bundled him out into the night.

Malgas stood for an age in a canted doorway, watching, waiting, while Nieuwenhuizen gathered wood and built a fire, cooked a rabbit, ate it with relish, and sat on a stone nodding off and mumbling a camp-fire lullaby. Then he turned his back on the tableau and ranged wearily through the dim ruins, marvelling at the debris, the balanced bits and pieces, above all, the incongruous juxtapositions, which he listed thus quietly to himself: hat and hammer, rock and paper, headache pill and custard powder, book and trousers, pipe and key, sealing-wax and vacuum cleaner, + and – until he tired of the game. He started on a list of miraculous survivors: light-bulb . . . and left it there. He dared not go upstairs: the grand staircase hung by a thread and a nail. He went instead into his room and lay down on the rug, with his head against his toolbox. His hips ached. He shut his eyes, but sleep would not come.

Hip, the house was tossing and turning, its rooms were banging together in the dark. A button sprang off the belly of an armchair and ricocheted, hip, hip, louder and louder, hurrah. Threads unravelled noisily. Whirlwinds swirled out of teacups and ripped through paper bags. Hooray! Portraits of Nieuwenhuizen's ancestors fell from the walls. Hip, hip, joints disjointed and screws unscrewed, plugs unplugged and locks unlocked, and so on and so forth, hubba hubba, the whole place was coming unstuck. Malgas tossed and turned with the tide *en nog 'n piep.*

The grand staircase slipped sideways and vanished in a chattering flight of planks and nails. Malgas crept under the scraps of the rug and pulled them tight around him, while fragments of house rained down on him and rebounded into the void. He heard voices whispering, wind howling, machinery clanking. He saw the familiar silhouette of his old rooftop, and Mrs in a frame of amber light, impossibly distant.

Then the house began to flicker and flare, and parts of it flapped away into the night, and parts of it crumpled up like sheets of paper. Malgas was scrunched up and folded flat, and pressed down into the ground with the house.

Time passed.

When the dead hand of the night lay on the small hours of the morning, Malgas lunged into a state of brilliant wakefulness. The air was roaring. It sounded like a torrent of voices, but it was coming from his blood and the heaving walls. The house was trying to pull itself together. Malgas struggled to his feet in the flow. He grunted and groaned with the house, and it breathed him in and out, and it sweated him and bled him and made him ache. Then the air turned to dish-water, as if the dawn had sprung a leak. Colour blazed up in the walls, swept through the ruins, and filled the creased spaces with sunshine.

Malgas gambolled in the light and gulped it down in greedy mouthfuls. The light foamed in his blood, and spangled it, and his veins were filled with sparkling music. Then the sweetness curdled as the house began to crack open and drift apart. Malgas called out to the parts that were precious to him, and grasped them lightly by their names, cradled them on his tongue for a moment and rolled them over his taste-buds for old times' sake, before they slipped from his lips, losing their colours, fading into forgetfulness.

The house was full of holes and the night poured in. The rafters turned to charcoal, the roof crashed down onto the observation deck, and that crashed down onto the floor below. Flocks of nails flew up into the sky. Storey after storey, amid clouds of dust and laughter, the house fell in on itself. The walls flared up and faded, and died down, now flaring up again – guttering –

The world drained out of Malgas. On an empty screen a single nail revolved into an exquisitely formed full stop.

Malgas was struck dumb. He fell down in a stupor, and the new house fell down with him, at last. Crash.

Mrs Malgas spent the night at the window.

The arrival of the removers annoyed her (she felt left out, of course) and she considered phoning the police. But watching the four of them stumbling around, breaking things and tripping over one another, and listening to their chorus of thuds and curses, had a surprising effect on her: she began to find them amusing. It's not funny, she told herself, and stifled a giggle. Just then Nieuwenhuizen dropped a barbell on his foot, and although he laughed it off and said he felt no pain, Mr started whimpering on his behalf. The removers tittered behind their caps. It's laughable, Mrs corrected herself, and laughed out loud. She laughed and laughed; she hadn't laughed so much in years.

Later, when the removers sat on the pavement warming themselves at a brazier and drinking, while Mr rose and fell in a delirium of terror and remorse, she tasted bubbles of laughter in the back of her throat again. But when cars began to coast up with their headlights off, and figures were gathering themselves into groups, their voices coming and going, their eyes turning in, the lenses of their glasses flashing secret messages through the grainy air, her throat dried up.

People are beginning to stare, she thought, and waited grimly for morning.

．　．　．

The puckered eaves of the Malgases' house lent an inquisitive expression to its normally bored face. This slight transformation irked Nieuwenhuizen, who was preparing to retire and looking forward to an uneventful sleep.

He thought he saw Mrs backing away from the lounge window looking over her shoulder, but it seemed to him that she was no more than a mote in a blind eye. He saw Mr too, closer to home, and found him for the moment incomprehensible, like a joke without a punch line.

Under the malignant influence of these thoughts Nieuwenhuizen concluded with a world-weary sonority that got on his own nerves: "We are condemned to renounce and repeat, the head and the tail, the one barking and the other wagging, with the body of the same old dog between them."

And fell fast asleep.

Mr Malgas lay like a victim of the ongoing violence in a shallow grave. Words trickled through him and seeped away into the sand. The night held a hand on the nape of his neck, and whenever he was buoyed up by a familiar intonation or an inspiring turn of phrase, that hand pressed him down again.

Conspiracy. Consanguinity. Contrariety. Confundity. Conundrumbrage.

He thought he felt boots treading the small of his back and the tops of his thighs, embossing him with algebra and etymology. Footsteps thundered in his chest cavity. Later, fingers of light brushed over him and he rose to the surface and knocked against the earth's meniscus. As he floated there a voice began to call him insistently, Malgas, Malgas, caught its sibilant hooks in the fabric of his skin, and reeled him, thrashing, upwards. His head, which was bloated with stuffy air and numbed by the echoes of his name, cracked through the crust. He looked at the foreign landscape under his nose.

Daybreak. His head rolled over. A cruet-stand came into view – salt and pepper tom-toms and a mustard-pot in the shape of a mud hut. Behind the hut the legs of a lectern rose like three slender tree trunks; and behind the trees, dwarfing them, the mirrored face of a wardrobe as tall as a skyscraper. Behind the tower block, against the grey sky, far-away mountains assumed the shape of his house. In that instant of recognition, his whole body solidified in a rush of blood and he crashed into the air.

He rolled over onto his back. Flopping his head from side to side, he took in the wreckage: furniture, clothing, bric-à-brac, kitchen-ware, toiletries. What was that sound? Water running. A broken pipe . . . no, never. "I imagined it all," he told himself firmly. "None of it was real. Except for this jumble of junk and cheap packaging. I wonder what became of the removers? Not to mention Otto."

Mr Malgas sat up, and the people gathered in the street on the edge of the plot burbled their approval. He wiped the sleep out of his eyes and focused on them. They were making a noise, babbling like water over stones, empty shells clacking together in the backwash.

When they felt the light touch of his attention upon them, the members of the crowd asserted their individual personalities and shapes by passing comments and thrusting out their chests to show the colourful labels and pithy slogans on their clothing, but they spoilt the effect by all speaking at the same time and pressing together in a mass, shoulder to shoulder and belly to back.

Malgas squinted. No doubt about it. There were hundreds of them, people, held back by festoons of candy-striped ribbon and paper-chains of policemen. Bright lights on tall tripods looked over their shoulders, and beyond them other lights winked on the roofs of cars and trucks, and glinted on scaffolds and catwalks.

Mr Malgas stared at the people. The people fell silent, in dribs and drabs, and stared back.

There were faces he knew, scattered among the popping flash bulbs, partly obscured by cameras. Mrs Dworkin, a couple of waitresses, one of the grillers, and Van As, the storeman. Bob and Alison Parker, also of the Helpmekaar – they had the stationery shop next to the escalators. Dinnerstein. The Greek from the corner café. Some relatives of Mrs from the coast. Venter, her gluttonous second cousin. There were friends and neighbours – Long time no see! – some stalwarts of the Civil Defence League, the Treasurer of the Ratepayers' Association, what was his name? . . . De Lange. There were customers and clients, Benny Buys in his Mr Hardware T-shirt, children, grandchildren, nephews, nieces and sales representatives. The postman. The removers, surrounded by photographers (news and fashion). Doctors and nurses, lawyers, electrical engineers, interior decorators, miners, market gardeners, cashiers, taxi-drivers and supermarket packers (to name just a few). There were dozens of nodding acquaintances, they were smiling and nodding their heads, but their names escaped him. There were countless others, who were bound to be strangers. There were thousands lost to sight and millions – no, *billions* entirely absent! And beyond them all, the vast and silent majority of the dead and the yet to be conceived.

For some reason this speculative train of thought reassured Mr Malgas and, for reasons that were easier to grasp, reminded him of Nieuwenhuizen. He got to his feet. The crowd cheered his effort generously. He was aching from head to toe, and he winced and grumbled to himself as he picked his way through the debris to the camp. The cameras captured the tiniest twinge and magnified it; the microphones mopped up the softest groan and amplified it.

The tent was still standing, and Nieuwenhuizen was inside it sleeping like a log. His untroubled breathing rippled the canvas walls and enlivened the guy-ropes. Mr Malgas thought he would wake him with a cup of tea. He found the gas-bottle gizmo and the bottle itself among the clutter at the foot of the tree; he found the pot jammed into the hedge; but he couldn't find water. The drum was empty. While he was checking the pots and jars for water, the zip grated open and Nieuwenhuizen stuck out his head.

The people responded with a breath-taking display of shimmering palms and flashing bulbs.

Nieuwenhuizen took in the situation at a glance. "Who are these people, Malgas?"

"It's the wider society."

"You don't say."

Nieuwenhuizen squirmed through the flap and clattered to his feet. The crowd cheered and surged against the barriers. Nieuwenhuizen dug up a pair of field-glasses and surveyed the crowd.

"Ridiculous," Mr Malgas thought. "He can call them field-glasses if he likes. But I say it's two brown beer bottles tied together with wire."

"Hm, you're right," Nieuwenhuizen said. "It is them. The people. Office-bearers and ordinary ones. A good smear of thrill-seekers too, I should say. Motor cars. Must belong to them. Buses, yes, mini- and tour-. What's this? Television aerials, roof-tops, steeples. It's the outside world all right. I might have known they'd turn up eventually, and just in time to be too late."

"I could find out what they want."

"Thanks, but that won't be necessary. I'll just pack a few things, and then we can have one for the road and a little chat."

Nieuwenhuizen unearthed the portmanteau from under a pile of driftwood, gathered up a few items – the hurricane-lamp, the two-legged pot, the nail – and crept back into the tent.

The crowd lapped at the barriers and fell back with a collective sigh.

Mrs ate her cornflakes in front of the TV set. She saw Nieuwenhuizen and Mr on the news update, sitting on stones in front of the tent, staring into the ashes and talking. There were close-ups of their mouths moving, and she wished that she could lip-read. There were shots of their faces – His was full of bruised shadows and dotted lines – and their hands, clutching crooked knives and forks, dented mugs and paper plates, all empty.

Then the camera withdrew to a discreet distance and panned over the site, fingering Nieuwenhuizen's broken-down furniture and personal possessions. His household effects looked pathetic out in the open, covered with frost, in the public eye. Where had all these people come from? What did they want? The camera read her mind, and showed her the eager expressions of the crowd, and then His old-fashioned ornaments trampled into the ground. There was a china shoe that looked familiar, a five and a half, a vase in the shape of a swan, a pretty tea-set, a porcelain figurine of a woman caught in the rain, a matchbox-holder with the crest of a seaside municipality on it. What were these trifles doing on the news?

"Why are we waiting? Why are we waiting?"

Mrs turned away from the tiny spectacle, walked to the window, and looked at the real-life drama. There you are.

Bucket, two-litre, red, plastic. Starfish (echinoderm), five-legged (six?), pink, dormant. Spade, blue, plastic. *Ex unitate vires.*

Then Mrs Malgas went down the garden path carrying a tray loaded with two plates of bacon, crispy, and eggs, sunny side up, two mugs (I ♥ DIY for Mr and the frog-mug for Him), tea-bags, a sugar-bowl, a thermos flask full of hot water, knives and forks, salt and pepper, tomato sauce in a plastic tomato, Worcester sauce in a plastic tower of Babel, and a sheaf of serviettes. In a shopping-basket over her shoulder were chocolate bars and packets of boiled sweets, waterproof sachets of Toppers and Smash, wads of cotton wool, a tube of Guronsan C, a bottle of disinfectant and a box of plasters (26 strips, 8 patches and 16 spots).

"Why are we waiting? It's getting irritating!" The crowd struck up a slow handclap to accompany the chant. She plunged in, the crowd parted miraculously in front of the steaming plates, and she came up against the barrier. A policeman tried to stop her from going further by pinching her arm, but she told him sternly, he was young enough to be her son, "That's my husband Mr and his chum Otto. Make way."

She ducked under the barrier and advanced towards the camp. A ripple of excitement washed through the crowd and the chanting quickened. It was all she could do not to break into a run. The ground underfoot had the consistency of a ripe Brie and it clung to her woolly slippers. She picked her way through a minefield of knick-knacks, and as she passed she tried to remember where the duck was, the pottery mallard, and the guineafowl with sunflower-seed feathers, and the pine-cone owl and the ostrich-egg representation of the Golden City.

Mrs Malgas's entry onto the plot was a model of dignity and restraint: she walked cautiously but purposefully, with her head held high and her shoulders thrust back. Her sequinned gown rippled like sunlit water. Mr Malgas got to his feet and looked at her in amazement. She went on steadily, bringing to bear on her trembling limbs every precept of self-defence in dangerous neighbourhoods. Yet all the human dignity she could muster mattered not a jot to the crowd, who took her long-overdue appearance as a signal that the forbidden territory was no longer out of bounds. They rose up in a foment of curiosity and acquisitiveness, and surged forward, carrying the barriers and the policemen along with them.

Mrs looked over her shoulder and froze in an attitude of disbelief as the crowd swept down upon her. Mr himself stood rooted to the spot, with Nieuwenhuizen's last words drumming in his ears. Nieuwenhuizen, on the other hand, got calmly to his feet in the face of the flood, as if he had done it all before, seized his portmanteau and executed a death-defying leap into the branches of the tree. He forked his limbs, spread his fingers, and in the twinkling of an eye was lost to sight.

The onrushing crowd fell upon the scene and carried off what they could. Mrs was knocked flat. At the last moment Mr came to life. He began scooping up gadgets, with a half-formed notion in his mind that they were of historical significance. Unfortunately this ill-considered action drew attention to these objects, which might otherwise have escaped notice, and endowed them with a special importance, and the crowd set upon him to rob him of his loot.

When it was all over, when the camp had been stripped of everything of value and a lot of rubbish besides, the crowd receded, bearing away its own wounded, and leaving behind a little wreckage, rags and kindling. Mr too remained behind, marooned, under a scrap of canvas fluttering from a wooden post.

Mrs found him there. "I've saved some of the doodads," she said, to cheer him up.

"No, no," he said, taking her basket from her and emptying the dead birds out on the ground. "He's lost everything, but he's resigned to it, and so am I."

She took the flag from him and laid it aside. She took his soft, ungiving hand in her own and led him home, and bathed him, and dried him and powdered him, and put him to bed like a baby.

"It's good to lie in my own bed again." He touched her salty cheek and dropped off.

Mr sniffed. Wood-smoke? He went to the window. Nieuwenhuizen was picking through the jetsam and tossing things into the fire. Mr willed him to look up, and wave, but he would not.

"Come away from the window," said Mrs, spooning two eggs into a pot of boiling water and inverting the egg-timer.

Mr sat down at the table and sighed heavily. "I'm sorry Mrs. There, I've said it."

"There's no need to apologize. I'm just grateful you've come to your senses while we've still got a roof over our heads and food on the table. Thank heavens everything's back to normal."

"We're back where we started . . . but let's not pretend that things are the same."

"Words, words, words," said Mrs, misunderstanding him. "Let's not pretend at all. It doesn't suit us. Let's just get on with our lives."

"Fine by me."

"Shame. You'll get over it. One day we'll look back on all this and discover that we can laugh about it."

"I can laugh about it already." He produced a hollow belly-laugh as proof.

"Me too. Now eat your egg before it gets cold."

"He was walking up and down all day like a vacuum cleaner," Mrs told Mr that evening when he came in from work. "First he picked up all his bits and pieces, and he put some of them into his suitcase and he put the rest on a pile. Then he broke the big bits he didn't want into smaller bits and burned them. The smell! He dug a big hole with that spade you lent him, which he never had the decency to return, and he buried all the bits that wouldn't burn. Everything fitted. But he tamped it down anyway with a wooden post, and then he threw the post over the hedge. He filled in the hole with the ashes and the sand he'd dug out to begin with. He beat the sand down, so that it was flat and smooth. He sprinkled more sand and small stones. Then he walked backwards, from one end to the other, brushing the earth with a branch and sowing handfuls of twigs no larger than ladyfingers. When he was finished there was no sign of him left."

"He's still there," said Mr, wiping a porthole in the misted glass.

"No he's not. He left long ago."

Mr and Mrs thought there would be something about him on the news, but they were mistaken.

"It's too early."

"It's too late."

. . .

The sun sank. Nieuwenhuizen looked at the wall and at the house. Perhaps it was a trick of the light, but even as the sun dropped behind the Malgases' roof, the suns in their wall sent out a host of lack-lustre rays, which got longer and longer, so that they appeared to be rising.

Nieuwenhuizen picked up the portmanteau and found his way to the edge of the plot. He sat on the verge, in the fallen darkness, holding up one finger, looking down the street.

archipelago books

is a not-for-profit literary press devoted to
promoting cross-cultural exchange through innovative
classic and contemporary international literature
www.archipelagobooks.org